# Ripple in Still Waters

Monique Champagne

NEWMAN SPRINGS PUBLISHING
320 Broad Street
Red Bank, NJ 07701

First originally published by Newman Springs Publishing 2019

ISBN 978-1-64531-550-6 (Paperback)
ISBN 978-1-64531-551-3 (Digital)

Printed in the United States of America

In memory of Michelle

May this book bring comfort and help to someone somewhere.

May you always have hope and never stop praying, and never *ever* lose faith, because God is real. This book will maybe touch someone in some way to accept the things we cannot change and to accept that our free will is a gift; it isn't always the final say. Freedom of choice is a blessing, and a curse.

May this story penetrate the readers' hearts, so they feel God's love within, and his power and strength, lighten the burdens of life, and enjoy its benefits. And believe! It makes all the difference. Let's make a difference and spread his love to everyone! His powers are ours for the taking, just believe.

# *Acknowledgments*

To my Mom Doris, my best friend,
and to my Dad, Marcel J, RIP,
and to my sweetest, dearest,
darling Donald, Thank you for
EVERYTHING!

This book was written to prove God and to glorify his name. This is his book. His persistence and guidance led me to write this book. Without God, this book would not exist.

I hope that his book will bring some comfort and help someone somewhere, to always have hope, and never stop praying, and never lose faith.

I hope that this book will maybe touch them in some way, to accept the things we cannot change, and to accept that our own free will is a gift, and it isn't always the final say, and freedom of choice is a blessing and a curse.

May this story penetrate the readers' hearts, so they feel God's love within, and lighten the burdens of life and enjoy its benefits.

# *Character List*

Martha Disolets—mother
Tony Disolets—father
Donny Disolets—oldest son
Tommy Disolets—younger son
Tori Disolets—first daughter, deceased
Fiona Disolets—youngest daughter, last child
Mickey Melouin—Fiona's school dropout boyfriend, abusive, drugs, arrests
Rachael Johnson—Fiona's best friend
Sequoia Matthews—Fiona's tag-a-long friend, Mickey's secret mistress

Fiona's new friends in California:

Sly—The recruiter. A puppet to Buzz, a school dropout who can't read or write, only knows street life, never knew love. Creepy-looking, scraggly-haired with beady eyes. Works by night, sleeps by day. Fiona met him first, and he offered her a place to stay, and in exchange, Fiona sells cocaine for him. Sly introduces her to the top guy, Buzz, and she becomes his number-one girl.

Buzz—Fiona's pimp who renamed her Scarlett, a drug pusher, dangerous, with a network of mules to move his goods in any district. Another school dropout who can't read or write. Tall, dark, and handsome, husky and strong, living a life of crime. Buzz has hits on people who didn't pay up or crossed him in some way.

Rafael—The bodyguard for Buzz and Scarlett, 100 percent loyal to Buzz, all muscle, and with a big square head, like a bucket, with nothing in it, and empty eyes. If people don't pay up, he breaks their heads, arms, legs, etc.

# *Chapter 1*

THE SUMMER OF AUGUST '66 came and went like a gentle breeze, passing by like the blink of an eye.

Fiona, now two years old, was a handful for her mother Martha, who was still mourning her first daughter, Tori, who passed away in 1962. Martha was left fervently perplexed. If it wasn't for Martha's strong faith, Tori's death would've destroyed her.

Martha's mind always wandered and drifted back to the past, before Fiona, before Tori. Martha's memories began to flood her mind as she remembered when she and Tony first started out together. Her mind took her to the beginning of it all.

Martha Doucette was born in 1932, in New Brunswick, Canada, in the maritime area, and raised by the sea. She moved to the United States, to Massachusetts, as she followed the East Coast, to find work and start a new life. She found herself a good job at Mead Paper, and then became a US citizen.

Martha was tall and slender, and had a face like a china doll. She turned heads, which always made her uncomfortable. She was a real go-getter with dreams and goals.

Tony Disolets worked for Mead Paper as well, and that's where they met. They had so much in common that they never ran out of things to talk about, sometimes speaking in French. Tony was also an immigrant from Canada, but he was from a tiny little farm in a tiny little town in St. Samuel, Quebec, Canada. But Tony was only eight years old when his family left the farm and came to America. He became a US citizen as soon as he could. He didn't think it was ethical to use two countries.

Martha was introduced to Tony's entire family (nine kids), and they were crazy about her. Martha didn't feel so homesick being accepted by Tony's family. Martha and Tony married in 1955. Her memories skipped right over the wedding, and jumped to when they had their first child right away, a son, Donald Disolets. Fifteen months later, they had another son, Thomas Disolets.

Martha was an excellent mother and wife. She took both roles very seriously. Tony was rather handsome with his jet-black hair and dark brown eyes. He was faithful to his exercises with Jack La Lain. Tony had a deep voice and an awesome, contagious laugh. He was famous for his jokes. But Tony had never forgotten about the tough times he had growing up.

When he was eighteen, he almost died. His goiter had to come out and he almost bled to death during surgery, so they had to operate in two sessions. They had to wait at least one month before they could finish the procedure. But in the meantime, Tony's neck was not allowed to heal completely and they would peel off any new skin growth, and then hold his neck together with butterfly clips.

Ten years later, at age twenty-eight, he became a very bad diabetic. It took over his life. Illness overshadowed his life now and in the years to come. Tony was dignified, and proud, and he was a perfectionist. He was a great provider and king of his castle. His boys meant the world to him.

Martha's memories now shifted to her children.

Donald, the oldest, was on the quiet side. He was a thinker, a listener. He was very smart, and he loved school. Donald was also dark and handsome like his father, Tony. Donald was pleasant and polite, and always did what he was told. Fifteen months later, they had another son, Thomas.

Thomas was a little clown, always trying to get laughs. One son serious and quiet, and the other loud and funny. Tommy was a real prankster and a big teaser. Never serious. He too had his father's contagious laugh and great smile. He was always eager to pull something off every chance he could, just to see what he could get away with. He loved to trick people. He was always happy, a real delight to have around, always loveable. Everybody's buddy.

Looking back, Martha now remembered 1960. Tommy was only two-and-a-half years old when his sister Tori was born. And Donald had just turned four years old.

Martha and Tony were so excited to finally have their little girl, especially Martha. They were devastated to learn that Tori had an inoperable heart defect and Down syndrome, and she wasn't supposed to make it out of the hospital. Martha cried her eyes out, and Tony was lost for words. Nothing he could say would make it better. He drowned himself in his work and got a big promotion and a transfer to James River Paper, as a foreman, a salary position.

Martha became a full-time mom. Back then, Tommy was still small enough to run into Tori's room and climb right up and over the rail and into her crib. He would get so excited to see her and would tickle her until her laughter turned into choking and gasping for air. Of course, Martha came to her rescue every time. Martha would pick Tori up high over her head and out of that crib, checking Tori's blueness in her face and waiting for her normal paleness to return; all the while Tommy would be jumping on the crib mattress trying to bounce higher and higher every time, giggling each time as he tried to hold onto the railing while trying to give Tori little kisses on top of her head every time he bounced back down.

"Okay, okay, that's enough, silly man," Martha would say, and she would always scoop him up with her free arm out of the crib and onto the floor he would go, running as soon as those little feet hit the floor, reminding Martha of those little toy cars that you have to wind up a few times before letting it go and watch it zoom away on its own. Martha was caught up in her memories of the past, remembering before Fiona, when Tori was still alive. Martha always cuddled baby Tori with such tenderness. But the everyday fear of losing Tori, and the *will this be the day* thinking was always eating at Martha; she could hardly bear it. Even though Tommy was screaming and playing and jumping around and yelling, Martha didn't comprehend the noise. She couldn't hear a thing where her mind drifted off to, existing far and deep into her thoughts within her mind. She rocked that baby constantly, doing all she could to comfort Tori when she had difficulty breathing, which became more frequent and Martha knew it. And that's what troubled her; she felt so alone at times. Two young boys, ages four and two, almost three, and now her little girl Tori, who was so sick and wasn't supposed to live more than a week. But God, in all his love and kindness and perfectness, sent Tori to the best mother he knew of for her. He blessed her in that way. And on October 2, 1961, Tori had her first birthday, which nobody ever thought she'd live to see. That just goes to show you what love can do. Tori was surrounded by love.

All these memories flooded Martha's mind as she ran after Fiona playing outside. Fiona may be two now, but she is lively and needs to be watched every second. Martha left the memories and realized she was sitting in the sun watching Fiona play.

And then her mind drifted off once again to the memories of Tori, when she was still living. And the memories started right where they left off, although the memories never left her mind.

Martha grew tired, and tired of knowing that the doctors had told her that there wasn't anything they could do, thinking all the way back to 1960.

"That black miserable day of Tori's death will surely come prematurely," the doctor said, "without a doubt, there isn't a cure for this type of heart defect. Medicine hasn't gotten that far," he explained. That's all Martha could hear in her mind over and over and over again.

The doctor also told them that all they could do was keep her comfortable and let her know that she is loved. And since that day that he told them these words, it seemed to be the only thing Martha could hear playing over and over and over again in her head. She wanted to scream! And cry. She could never seem to shut it off or turn it down. This poor woman's pain was unbearable, anyone could see the pain all over her face, even today.

Martha cherished her time with Fiona, now playing in the sandbox in the backyard shade. And then Martha's mind returns to her memories, right where she left off.

"Martha, are you alright?" Tony yelled out to her.

But she couldn't hear him in her deep thoughts and did not respond. "Martha!" he yelled out to her again, as she rocked the baby so slowly and stared into space as though in a trance. "For Christ's sakes, Martha!" Tony yelled at the top of his lungs.

"What?" she asked in almost a whisper.

"Can't you see that Tommy is running around like a loose animal that belongs in the zoo? Obviously you did not even know where Tommy was because you're in a daze again! Well, he snuck into our bedroom while I was asleep and hit me over the head with the metal Tonka truck! What a way to wake up! I must have a black eye! I *was* asleep! I have to get some sleep if I am going to work swing shifts!" Tony continued. "Martha, you got to get a grip! I have to sleep if I'm supposed to work around the clock. You have to be there for the boys too, you know," Tony ranted.

So Martha, staying ever so calm, stood up to get out of the rocking chair. She walked over to Tony, and as she stared into her husband's eyes, she handed him the dying baby.

There was so much that she wanted to say to him, and yet, where to begin? She had so much emotion bottled up inside her. But she chose to remain silent, and her actions spoke louder than words could have, and absolutely said it all. Tony was speechless. He got the point.

"Come on, boys," she yelled as she motioned them to follow her, "what do you say we make some pancakes for breakfast?" She knew it was their favorite.

"Yeah!" the boys shouted as they raced each other to the kitchen. The messier they got, the more they liked it. They cherished having mommy's attention all to themselves, but they never fussed when she was busy with Tori. Without understanding all the facts, somehow these two little brothers knew she came first. They knew something wasn't right. And in waiting their turn for attention, that was their way of helping.

"I want to stir," Tommy said.

"Well then, I'm pouring the pancakes. Mom, tell him," Donald said in a frustrated voice.

"That's fine," Martha said as she got her head out of the clouds once again, daydreaming about her life before kids.

Martha had another memory about when she herself was a child. There were twelve kids in all, and they would get so excited when their mother, Elise, would make them some black butter, they called it, for a treat. And it was just butter and cocoa. It was the only sweet thing they had, growing up so poor.

Living next to the ocean was only nice in the warmer months; in the winter, they nearly froze. They probably would have frozen if they didn't sleep three in a bed. The beds that they had to re-stuff with straw or hay every summer. There wasn't much they could afford.

Martha was the third child of twelve, third child just like Tori. Then she pictured her father, when he would come home from trapping, hunting, or fishing, and then back out on another trip. He was gone more than he was home.

She remembered that they had a garden and chickens in the coop, fresh eggs every day. Each child had only one outfit. Some had shoes. People in the community felt so bad for all of them being left to fend for themselves and how their lives were a struggle. The kids were so thin. The community would donate clothes and sometimes food.

And everyone adored Martha's mother, Elise. She was so pleasantly happy and loving, and trusted God in everything. She passed her faith down to her children so they would have it for life and know God and right from wrong. All you had to do was take one look at her to know the Holy Spirit dwelled within her.

Martha always missed her mother terribly, especially in hard times, even as a grown mother of three. And with that thought, Martha began to hear the boys in the background as they fussed at each other, again in her other memories. A memory within a memory.

"No! Not yet! I'm not done stirring!" Tommy cried. "Mom! Tell him to wait!" "Okay, Donald," Martha said, "he's just about done, he has five more stirs. Are you guys ready? Let's count together." And as Tommy stirred the pancake mix, the three of them counted out loud together.

"One, two, three, four, five!" they all yelled at the same time. And then they laughed. In an instant, Tommy jumped off the kitchen chair he was standing on and ran into the living room where Tony was rocking Tori.

Donny stood on a kitchen chair reaching over to hug his mother, and then he began pouring the pancake batter onto the hot griddle.

"I love you, Mommy," Donny said as he winked at Martha playfully.

And Tommy was back in the kitchen running around yelling, "Yeah, mommy, me too!"

Martha yelled back that she loved them too as her eyes welled up with tears. She could hear Tori fussing and crying from the living room and figured Tony probably needed a break, and Tori too for that matter. Tony was nervous not knowing what to do for her. So since Martha couldn't eat anything if she tried, she figured she would free up Tony from pacing around the room quieting Tori, and let him enjoy some pancakes with the boys.

"I hope you're hungry? I made plenty," she told him as she entered the room. "Oh boy! I could eat. Thanks, honey, I love you."

"Yeah, I love you too, Tony," she replied as he handed her the baby. Instantly, Tori stopped crying and fussing as her mother's tender touch calmed her.

Martha's thoughts dissipated and she suddenly realized she was in the backyard, by the pool, watching Fiona play in the sandbox in the shade. And the boys were right here with her too, splashing each other in the pool. Martha savored the moment.

But then she slowly drifted right back to her memories of earlier times, when Tori was still alive. Her thoughts brought her back to 1960, the year Tori was born. It was almost like reliving the heartache all over again.

Martha's memories brought her back to Halloween time 1960. It was only a week away, and Martha didn't know how she was going to make the boys' costumes this year.

Tony already had planned to bring the boys to pick something out, whatever costume they wanted at Child World or Bradlees or Woolworths. He was going to tell Martha at the dinner table that evening.

She heard his car door shut in the garage and then the kitchen door opened as Tony walked through it.

He walked over to her and wrapped his arms around her as he pushed her hair back and out of her face and said, "I love you so much, honey. We will get through this."

Martha remembered how she pushed him away shouting *"Oh, I know, this too shall pass!"* with the sarcasm in her voice coming through loud and clear.

He knew she was in pain. He was too.

She sniffled as she grabbed for a tissue and then walked back over to him and said, "I love you too, but it hurts. Our poor little girl with both a heart defect and Down syndrome to boot!" She raised her voice in anger. The couple embraced, holding each other tightly as they clung to whatever little hope was left.

"I have a surprise for you, Martha. I am going to take the boys with me to Howard Johnson's Restaurant for supper tonight, and then shopping for Halloween costumes.

That'll give you and Tori some alone time together. Maybe we can fit a cozy bubble bath in your future this evening. Aaand…" he said with a long stretch and a sweet smile, "I'll bring you back anything you want for supper. How's *that* sound?"

She sighed with relief as she wiped her tears and said, "I would love some wonton soup."

"Wonton soup it is!" Tony replied cheerfully.

The boys came flying out of the playroom racing each other. When Dad told them the news about going costume shopping, they started running in a circle with excitement and then ran off into the living room, diving into the furniture.

"I think they're happy," Martha blurted as the couple giggled together.

"All right, you guys, get your boots on and your coats, I'm ready," Tony told them.

"Use the bathroom first, it's a long ride," Martha yelled.

Donny and Tommy did what they were told.

Tony grabbed Martha around the waist and held her close and told her with all sincerity, "We will get through this, I'll miss her too, I love her. She's my little angel. But we have to prepare ourselves and keep it together, because the day is coming faster than we think, I can feel it," Tony said, sobbing and reaching for his back pocket for his handkerchief to wipe his tears and blow his nose.

"I know, I feel it too, especially when I see how hard she's struggling to breathe sometimes."

Tony could hardly understand her, she was sobbing so awfully with such a weakness in the pit of her stomach.

Martha's heart ached for Tori and her slow death. Heart-wrenching for the both of them, but it was a raw reality that they were going to have to face. Ready or not. But she just couldn't face it and fell to her knees.

"Stay strong with me, Martha, and for the boys. They need you. I need you." Tony helped her up and kissed her as the kids ran by them without a clue with their boots on and their coats fighting for the front seat. He hugged her and kissed her again and gently let her go and followed them to the garage and into the car, a celery-green Pontiac station wagon with a V8 engine under the hood. Tony was never too excited about the car, he thought it cramped his style.

But Martha loved it because it was very functional for a growing family, although Martha had her doubts about the growing family part, when they're about to lose their baby girl. She felt so helpless and hopeless, and just cried her heart out. She finally pulled herself together and thought, before Tori wakes up, now would be a good time for that bubble bath her husband was talking about. She had to clean herself up at this point. And Tori was sound asleep.

Martha remembered that she did enjoy that bubble bath and remembered she relaxed in the rocking chair in Tori's room where she watched how peaceful she looked as she slept. Her face glowed as though she could already get a glimpse of God. And Martha had to think that way. Who else better to end up with in God's arms?

A loud noise made Martha jump to her feet. Tony and the boys were back from the store and she thought to herself that was a fast trip. But when she looked at the clock, it was already eight o'clock. She couldn't believe that she was sitting in that rocker since five thirty. But it gave her some time to do some thinking and for that she was grateful. Her stomach had growled so loud with an endless rumble that she figured she better eat something today.

And there stood Tony in the doorway, holding a big plastic bag that read Woolworths on it, which must've been Halloween costumes for the kids, and he used his other hand to push open the door as he balanced her order of wonton soup.

Martha ran over to him to help him unload his arms. She was so grateful to him for remembering her soup. And that in itself made it a good reason to finally eat something. It was almost as though she would be able to let go of the pain she carried around always in the pit of her stomach.

It turned out to be a relaxing evening and a family night after all, Martha recalled. The boys always laid on the floor together while watching television. Martha always said they were like two worms. Always moving, wiggling, jumping, and squirming. Tony always laughed when he heard her describe them that way. There was no denying that it was a perfect description of the two little buggers.

Tori was content now in the baby swing, and Martha and Tony were stretched out together on the couch. They cherished this night knowing how fast things could change. Indeed they did.

Martha was upset that she had been dumb enough to let her guard down, because now that she did, trouble once again was knocking at the door, when Tori's health declined even more. This caused a ripple effect for Martha.

Martha swore that this was the last time she ever stopped worrying, because the minute she relaxed was when trouble really started. Tori wasn't coughing and choking anymore. In fact, Tori wasn't doing much of anything. And Tony and Martha got nervous and scared.

They decided that it would be best if Tony was the one to take her to the hospital and Martha would stay home with the boys, and she had them try on their costumes to distract them and herself from what was really taking place. Martha enjoyed the boys thoroughly that night. But the thought of Tori kept creeping into her mind, and she worried as her stomach churned.

Hours later, Tony returned from the hospital, but he was alone. Martha panicked, so Tony reassured her that everything was all right and they were keeping Tori overnight for observation. They wanted to give her some oxygen.

They both slept like rocks that night, even though Tony had informed Martha that it was, in fact, the beginning of the end for Tori. They had cried themselves to sleep, crying Tori tears.

The couple rose early the next morning feeling recharged and ready for what may lie ahead. Martha was ready first, and anxious to get to the hospital and pick up their little girl. She was usually last to be ready for the day, since she had to tend to Tori until the kids were off to day-care and kindergarten. Then she would have some time to herself.

When the couple returned home from the hospital, they both had very long faces. They'd been told by Tori's doctor that their precious little gem was dying. They'd thought that they were strong again and prepared and ready for anything today. But they weren't. They were devastated when they heard the doctor plainly say it to both of their faces. It cut like a knife to hear it out loud, and then to look at this beautiful little girl who was a gift from God and had always been on loan. They were like zombies walking around aimlessly and in circles, in a fog, in shock, absorbing facts, facing facts, as they tried to settle in.

Time marched on with daily routines. Halloween was a blur. Tony had taken the boys door to door in the neighborhood. It hit him hard when everyone wanted a Tori update. But he thought it might help him if he talked about her to the ones who asked. They all offered their prayers, and if they could help in any way, they were willing. It did make him feel a little better. He knew this was killing Martha. She was the one who was really coming undone. He didn't know how to help her. He was traveling this ugly road with her, and yet they had to walk it separately, and heal in their own way and their own time.

That awful day came when Tori ended up in the hospital again, and she wasn't coming home.

It was a blizzard the day Tori passed away, February 13, 1962. She was one year, four months, and eleven days old. Bless her soul, Tony's angel. They had given her only a week to live. What a trooper she was. See what love can do. Now she was in God's arms.

They humbly felt blessed to be the parents chosen by him to love her in all depths of life and death. And they most certainly did. But as much as Martha loved Tori, she could not get herself to go to the cemetery from the church the day of the funeral. It would take some time. She could not and would not stand by as they lowered her baby girl into the ground. The poor baby. How heart-wrenching for everyone.

"Why? Why?" Martha could hardly talk. She was so choked up. All the time. Even a year later, she was far away in her own thoughts. She would only speak when spoken to. It always seemed like she was someplace else. Most likely in the past, remembering Tori and everything about her. Replaying it over and over again like a bad dream. But it was real. And Martha was stuck, in a bad place. And Tony knew it.

Tony got some advice from their family physician. Tony told him that Martha wasn't talking or playing with their two sons or moving on since Tori's death. And the doctor told him that the couple should consider having another baby and hope to God that it's a girl. Tony thought about what the doctor had said. He wanted his house and everybody in it to get happy again and live on. He couldn't take all the gloom anymore.

Martha remembered how he approached her that night. He nonchalantly brushed on the subject of having another baby. He had pulled her to him while holding her arms behind her, then he ran his fingers across her shoulders and neck, and grabbed a handful of her dirty-blond hair as he held her head and pulled her close to himself, and began kissing her all over her body with lust and pure passion. Tony was heated up and ready for her. As he kissed her neck, she loosened up and became completely submissive to him as he entered her with all his love for her and all she'd been through. It had been a long time, and it was very emotional. He loved her so much he just wanted to give her another baby. And they both knew Martha was pregnant before he even pulled out of her.

She remembered how passionate Tony was as he held her in his tender loving arms, and how there were no words. They just cried together as they held each other. It was all understood between them. For the first time in a long time, they were on the same page. And then she thought about how it all seemed so long ago now. Tori's been gone for years now already. Fiona's conception happened on Tori's birthday (October 2, 1963), or on the anniversary of Tori's birthday (she would've been two).

And now Fiona was already two years old. Martha left her memories behind and became conscious of the present time, 1966. And Martha knew she had her hands full with this little girl of hers, Fiona. The good old days were just beginning.

# *Chapter 2*

WHEN FIONA WAS BARELY TWO years old, she gave Martha a mini stroke, pardon the expression.

Martha was yelling frantically in the distance, slowly becoming louder and louder, as she approached the old antique baby carriage that was in the neighbors' backyard, where she found Fiona pretending to be napping. She had snuck off without her mother Martha's knowledge.

Fiona lay quietly in that old antique baby carriage as she rubbed her hands across the soft white satin interior, as white as swans, curling up into a pink hand-crocheted blanket, giggling as though this were a game of hide and seek. Fiona laughed because she got away with it. And Mommy wasn't mad. No, Mommy was relieved.

Martha was always so overprotective since the loss of Tori. But Fiona didn't know anything about Tori. All Fiona knew was that she loved that old antique baby carriage from the moment she saw it the day before, when her mother walked over to the neighbors to say hello, as she held Fiona in her arms. That's when Fiona saw it for the first time and she decided that she would find a way to get in it. So, without hesitation, Tori snuck out to the neighbors the very next morning, wasting no time.

Martha had been up to her elbows in soapy, hot dishwater, doing the dishes at the kitchen sink. Fiona was surprised at how easy it was to sneak off quietly, although she had never tried anything like that before. She certainly did not foresee a ruckus. All she wanted was to get in that baby carriage, succeeding and cherishing every moment in that soft, plushy cocoon of hers.

Suddenly, her mother's face popped in to the opening of the carriage, scaring Fiona like a jack-in-the-box. Smiling and sighing with relief, Martha yelled to everyone looking for Fiona, "She's in here! She's okay! I found her!" Martha cried with relief as she bent down and picked up her little daughter gently, lifting her out of the snug hideaway. Fiona thought she would break, her mother hugged her so tight. From that day on, Martha never let Fiona out of her sight. But this choice caused a ripple effect.

Martha held on so tight all the time. It just made Fiona want to break free all the more. And that too caused many ripples in life's pond. And so the ball was rolling along with a spin of *I want to do it my way* from the get-go. From two years old on.

Whenever Fiona was asked to do one thing, she always managed to do just the opposite. One time, she walked barefoot on hot tar that had just been poured in the driveway of the new house when they first moved there.

They had just bought the house on a dead-end street with lots of kids for her kids to play with. It was a nice place to raise a young, growing family of three now that Tori passed. Martha could not bear to stay in the old house where Tori died. She was ready to move on now, she needed to.

When they moved, Martha wouldn't go until they changed the address number from a 13 (that damned 13th, Tori died on the 13th, the day before Valentine's Day), to an 11.

Fiona and her parents were sitting on the front porch of the new house the day they poured tar for the driveway. As the truck drove off, its bells were ringing and chiming loudly, and to Fiona it sounded happy, fun, and exciting. But she knew better than to go over to the hot driveway.

That is, until she heard her mother tell her father "You better watch her" in a stern voice.

And Tony replied, "Don't worry, she'll stay right here with us." So of course, Fiona took it as a dare and ran right over to the hot tar barefoot, completely unaware of what hot tar even was. Fiona managed to step right in it. Only then did she realize the consequences at hand.

Martha felt so blessed to be able to have a new start and for having this new little girl. She didn't take any of it for granted. She still missed Tori all the time, but vowed to let go of at least a little of the pain she'd been carrying so close to her for so long. It was time and she knew it. She could not do it anymore in that house where Tori died. She wouldn't stay in that house. Everything about it reminded her of Tori. And to Martha, all she had was memories and little reminders. She knew she could never move on unless they moved on to a new home, a new start. So they moved. That was when Fiona turned two years old. And the rest was history, as far as Martha was concerned. Because she, in fact, moved on. They all did.

And now, with summer of '66 almost over, and Fiona's feet almost healed, she couldn't wait for school to start. The boys would be gone all day at school, and Tony would be at work, and it would be just the girls at home all day.

Martha cherished all the one-on-one time she got to enjoy with healthy Fiona; they both healed. Fiona had become very attached to her mother at this point.

# *Chapter 3*

Tony always had to work swing shifts. It went with the foreman promotion at the paper mill. It was a pretty big accomplishment for someone who only finished the eighth grade before having to go to work. One week would be 11 p.m. to 7 a.m., one week would be 7 a.m. to 3 p.m., and the other shift was 3 p.m. to 11 p.m., and so forth, keeping the rotation every week.

Martha always worried about him with his diabetes. She never let him sleep too long, in fear of his sugar going through the roof, or even too low. She took very good care of Tony and the family. It was Martha's number-one priority.

Tony became a diabetic at his office Christmas party. He started rolling around in the snow, and everyone laughed thinking he was joking around and drunk, but he was having his first diabetic reaction in front of all those people. He almost went into a coma and stayed in the hospital for a week.

Tony tried so hard to give his family everything. He was even up to three jobs for a while. He always said, "If you don't have enough with one job, you get two, and if that isn't enough, you get three."

When it came time for Fiona to go to school, she was afraid to be apart from her mother, at first. And then she began to enjoy the sweet taste of independence. Fiona was only in kindergarten when she told the bus driver she wouldn't be going on the bus today, because her mommy would be picking her up.

Martha received a phone call from the Mother Superior at Julie Country Day School to inform her that Fiona was with her in the convent if she would like to come and pick her up. Martha was so embarrassed when she picked her up.

On the way home, she said to Fiona, "Fiona, you cannot just decide last minute if you are going to take the bus or if I am going to pick you up." She added calmly but sternly, "That has to be talked about before and decided already. You cannot just decide at school. What if I wasn't home? You'd still be at the convent"

"That's okay, Mama," Fiona replied, "those nuns were so nice, Mommy, they gave me a big juicy red apple and I got to sit in a really big chair that was made of wood and all shiny and the ceilings went to the sky and there was a statue of Jesus and Mary and Joseph everywhere!"

Martha drove them home laughing at Fiona's innocence. Then Martha told Fiona that if she ever did that again, she was going to make her become a nun, and Fiona laughed. Martha would love that. Then she thought that would be a dream come true, for her daughter to become a nun and run from all trouble. Then she wouldn't have to worry about her. But Martha was a worrier, about everything and anything, ever since the one time she let her guard down, when Tori ended up in the hospital.

Martha had finally relaxed for the evening, watching television with her husband and kids. And things started turning for the worse the one time she stopped worrying. She lived with guilt and a heaviness in her heart for being a hopeless case. But there really wasn't anything the doctors could do for Tori. She had a heart defect, and it was inoperable. And Martha knew deep down that Tori's death had absolutely nothing to do with her letting her guard down. It was all so complicated and heart-wrenching.

They finally pulled into the driveway and it seemed as though Fiona was out of the car and running to the house before Martha even had time to take the key out of the ignition.

Fiona ran to the family dog, Lazy, a beagle, who was crying with happiness and wagging her tail vigorously. There was a path which led to Tony's brother's house if you turned left. They didn't have children. They were neighbors and lived there long before Tony and Martha moved into the new neighborhood.

The kids would walk over to visit them. But when they came home, the dog followed and never left their sides since. Fiona and Lazy stuck together like glue. They would roam the backyard woods together. There was a path that led to Tony's brothers house. And if you turned right, it led to a penny candy store. After visiting the aunt and uncle, Fiona and Lazy would stop on the way home to nap together under the tall trees and cuddle each other as they would lay on the peat moss that fascinated Fiona.

Martha always got a phone call from them to let her know when Fiona was on her way back home. So if it was a long while, Martha would go looking for her and the dog, panicked, and then always relieved when she would find her lying down with Lazy under the tall trees on the peat moss, every time. But she couldn't help being worried knowing how spontaneous Fiona could be. Martha was overprotective after everything she had been through.

But Fiona knew nothing about the past of having an older sister before her, who had lived and died before she was ever born. And Martha had often pictured herself telling Fiona about Tori when the time was right. But that some time didn't come for some time, not until Fiona was about eight or nine years old. She overheard her parents talking about Tori, and she had heard that name before. So Fiona came right out and asked them who Tori was, so they told her about having an older sister, not knowing how she would react.

But Fiona got all excited and started jumping on the couch and yelling, "Show me some pictures! I want to see her."

For Martha this wasn't easy, since she had not talked about it since she promised herself to move on. But she didn't hold back. Martha got the old photo album out from the hallway closet and handed it over to Fiona.

She sat on the couch and started turning pages slowly. Fiona couldn't believe nobody had told her that she had a sister. And somehow, Fiona made it easier for the whole family to talk about Tori. It was like the eye of a needle, but it was an opening.

Over time, they all sort of opened up and told stories about those earlier days when Tori was still alive. And they did feel better, relieved that the family secret was out.

No more tiptoeing about it. It wasn't exactly a secret, but it had never been brought up.

The family was beginning to heal.

The boys were both in hockey and starting to like girls. Donny had his learner's permit. He was taking extra courses and working part-time at R. H. Whites, a fancy clothing store with fitted suits for men and women, and a tailor and everything. It was on the expensive side. Donny's mind was always preoccupied with his vision of this wonderful future he was going to have as soon as he got out of this little town. Better yet, he focused more on his vision of leaving this house and his bratty sister. If he had to put up with this much crap, he may as well just have his own damn family to put up with. Fiona drove him crazy. Good practice.

Tommy was always playing hockey. He loved the attention from all the girls. He even played hockey in the street, in front of the house. He would drag his hockey net with him and set it up across the street and continually practice his slap shots. Sometimes he would pretend to Fiona that he wanted her around, and he would talk her into being his goalie, and he would still practice his slap shots with all his force, and she was the target until she ran off crying with her feelings hurt more than anything. He laughed like hell every time she fell for it. But he loved her; he just couldn't admit it. They were very close. He just loved to tease her. And when enough was enough, he'd start with the dog.

Fiona had a busy schedule too. She took dancing lessons—tap, jazz, and ballet every Monday, Wednesday, and Friday. And she graduated from the brownies to the girl scouts, and took much pride in it. And she earned badges. And sold cookies. And took trips. And made arts and crafts. She was always doing something to earn another badge, always wanting more.

What seemed like days turned into years. Martha couldn't believe how fast time had gone by. The kids were growing so fast. But she was still uneasy since Tony told her that he wasn't feeling too good since becoming a diabetic, which is a whole other story.

His new boss had to call 911 and the ambulance took Tony away from the Christmas party. And that's when he found out he had diabetes. He had been so embarrassed, but everyone reassured him not to be silly. That's when he was twenty-eight years old. Right before Tori was born. But that was behind them now. All of it.

Martha had to make herself think of other things so she wouldn't end up in a depression. And time has passed now and has healed most wounds. This was the '70s. Donny was graduating high school. He was all set. He knew he wanted to go to UMASS and he was going to major in engineering. Fiona thought that meant he was going to drive a train. He dreamt of this chance his whole life. And his dreams did come true.

Tommy graduated high school in 1976, not in 1975. The school made him wait a year to start because his birthday was in January. After high school, he started a construction company and was successful.

Fiona was still in grade school, and anyone who ever met her new she had an older sister who died. When she reached the eighth grade, she graduated from girl scout to cadet. She had earned herself a trip selling cookies. The trip included the whole troop on a chartered bus, traveling the East Coast from Massachusetts to Disney World, Florida. There were many stops along the way. Fiona's most memorable stop besides Disney World was when she got to meet President Jimmy Carter. And they did some camping. She was away from home for two weeks on that trip, which helped her parents out immensely.

They had their own troubles back home. Tony was losing his eyesight from the diabetes. He decided to try surgery since laser treatments hadn't been the answer for him. He did have surgery on one eye.

When he and Martha went to pick up Fiona from her trip, he wore a big eye patch with lots of gauze under it. It was the first time Fiona even learned about him having an eye problem. The couple had always been very good at keeping their troubles from the kids.

Fiona ran to them both with arms wide open. She was glad to be back home. She'd never been gone that long before. She was very excited to be back, but she began to worry about her father. As they drove into the driveway when they arrived home, there was the dog, Lazy, waiting. Fiona's loyal companion. That dog jumped on Fiona as she cried with overwhelming joy.

"Lazy, hi, I missed you too!" Fiona replied as she held the dog tight. She gave her a kiss on the head, and then started running into the backyard with Lazy on her heels.

They must've ran around the pool ten times, as Lazy was just inches away from eating Fiona's heels, barking away like most beagles do. It was good to see the two of them so happy, and Fiona still innocent, at least for now.

Martha opened Tony's car door and helped him to the steps and into the house. "Why don't you relax in your recliner, honey, while I get something cooking for supper?"

"Okay by me," Tony answered. He closed his eyes and fell asleep. He was often tired these days. He was going through a lot. He was afraid that he would never see again. But ironically, he never talked about his fears. Deep down, he feared the worst. He knew he was feeling raunchy these days, and it had nothing to do with his eyes. But he always pushed it out of his mind to deny it. He looked so peaceful when he was asleep in his recliner. He loved that red vinyl recliner chair, even after Fiona almost ruined it.

It was kitty comer in the living room. And when Fiona was really little, she was small enough to sneak behind the chair. She had this fascination to punch holes through the back of the chair with a sharp pencil. She managed to poke holes in the entire back of the chair. It was a long time before her father caught her in the act. And was she *surprised!*

He knew he could hear a popping sound, like bubble wrap being popped. He thought he was going crazy. And when he stood up and flipped the chair around, he caught her red-handed.

"Get out of there now!" Tony shouted at her. "And don't *ever* let me catch you back there again!" And Fiona cried. Martha hadn't seen him this mad since he was hit

41

over the head with a metal Tonka truck while he was sleeping. That only happened once. Fiona never went behind that chair again either, or what was left of it at least.

Tony awoke when he heard Martha yelling through the screen door from the kitchen.

"Fiona! Time to come in now! Time to eat supper." But there was no reply.

Martha quickly shut off all the burners on the stove top and went outside with the screen door slamming. She walked to the backyard and started down the path that led to her in-laws' house (Tony's brother and his wife, the original owners of Lazy the dog). About halfway there, she spotted Fiona and Lazy asleep on a big patch of moss.

"Didn't you hear me calling for you, Fiona?"

"No, Mommy, sorry."

"All right, well, it's time for supper. Come on now."

"Okay, Mommy," Fiona replied as she got up and ran into the house with the beagle on her trail, inches from her heels, whipping the screen door open until it hit the railing on the porch.

"What the hell is going on out there?!" Tony shouted.

"It's just me, Daddy," Fiona answered.

"Take it easy for Christ's sakes, will you? You're going to break the damn door. I might not be able to see too good, but I sure as hell can hear!"

"Alright, Daddy, sorry," Fiona said as she ran into the bathroom slamming the door.

"What did I just get through saying?" Tony yelled, getting irritated and aggravated with her already. His eye hurt worse when he yelled.

"Oh yeah, sorry, Dad," she yelled back from the bathroom.

He heard the kitchen door close as Martha walked in.

"That must be you, Martha, I didn't hear a door slam," Tony rattled on sarcastically. "I don't know what we are going to do with her, she is such a live wire. She doesn't sit for a minute!"

"Nice switch, huh?" Martha mumbled. "Tony, you have to remember that these are the good old days." Then the two of them started laughing. "You wished for another girl, careful what you wish for." And they chuckled.

"Thanks, honey, I needed a good laugh. I feel much better now." And he smiled at her as he wondered if he was looking in the right direction. He couldn't see her. One eye was covered up with a patch, and the other one was blurry from laser treatments. Tony was praying that his eye surgery would help him to see. Even if just a little. He did not want to be dependent and completely blind. Suddenly he heard a noise in the hallway. It sounded like one of the Budweiser horses, but he could be wrong. It was only graceful Fiona coming out of the bathroom. *Fiona's fiasco,* he thought.

"Mom, I want to set the table, can I?" Fiona asked politely. "I just washed my hands," she continued.

"Sure," Martha said, "just try not to break the dishes," and she began to laugh. "Hey," Fiona said with disappointment in her voice. She didn't like to be teased. "We're just playing, Fee," Martha told her.

Fiona knew it and started giggling.

"Go get your father, tell him supper is ready."

43

"Dad, it's time to eat, hope you're hungry," Fiona told him as she grabbed his arm to help him out of his chair. As Fiona walked him to the kitchen, she started singing, "I'm leaving on a jet plane, I don't know when I'll be back again."

"All right, that's good," Tony told her, and they all sat down at the table. It was just the three of them tonight.

Donny was in college, and Tommy was working late. But they weren't missing anything. Supper consisted of corn, potatoes, and meatloaf with tomato soup gravy. It was all right, but nothing fancy.

"You know, Fiona," Tony said, teasing her, "that I have an appointment in Boston on March 2nd, 1978, of course. Your brothers aren't available to take me." Turning toward Martha, he asked, "Martha, do you think you could handle driving to Boston to take me to my doctor's appointment?" he asked nonchalantly, knowing the answer already. He just wanted to tease her.

"Are you kidding me, Tony? You know the answer to that!" Martha answered him excitedly.

"I know, honey, I don't even know why I brought it up."

"I'll bring you, Dad," Fiona practically shouted. She would love the chance to drive and to help out her dear ole dad. Daddy's girl would do anything she could for him, whatever, no matter what anyways. He was her best friend.

"Fiona, thanks, I knew you would if you could."

"I would if you'd let me, you mean. I almost have my learner's permit, Dad! And besides, who will know if we don't say anything?" Fiona pleaded.

Tony thought about it. Martha kept quiet because she wouldn't ever consider driving to Boston (and it wasn't as bad in the '70s), just the thought of it gave her anxiety.

"Well, if worse comes to worse, I suppose," Tony said. "We'll see. Bad choice of words," he continued under his breath. But Fiona really wanted to do this for him and she wouldn't let up.

"But, Dad," she said, "why did we spend the last couple of years practicing driving around the cemetery? I can take sharp comers. You even taught me how to drive a stick! You know I can drive. Come on, nobody will know! And besides, I am comfortable with it, and I know the way."

"Fine," he replied, letting out all the air in his lungs. "We'll have to call your school and sign you out for that day. If that's what it comes to."

"Thanks, Dad."

"I didn't say yes."

"I'll help you out, no problem," and she hurried and grabbed the phone off the wall on her way to the living room as she threw herself on the couch with her tiny dancer legs dangling off the arm of the couch. She had the phone cord stretched out to the max, and that always floored Tony. She dialed her best friend Rachael Johnson's number and filled her in about driving to Boston.

Tony overheard the conversation and shook his head and said, "No one will ever know, she says." Fiona could talk on the phone for hours, but when Tony got sick, she knew better than to tie up the line all the time.

# *Chapter 4*

Tony made it to his appointment on time. The doctor had told him that his eye was healing well. Tony knew it, because it always itched so bad. He already knew that it was a good sign. His eye was very irritating and he managed to handle it. He was given eye cream to help with the itching and that gritty sandpaper feel.

Then the doctor told him he could schedule his surgery for the other eye, if he was still interested.

He was satisfied with how the first eye was healing, but one more visit in a month will tell him if his vision was back to 20/20 or not. After going through laser treatments for a year, with surgery, he had his fingers crossed. So Tony agreed to go back in a month. He was happy with some good news for a change that everything was looking A-okay. It was a good boost for his morale, although he never saw well again. Mostly shadows.

He couldn't say enough about Fiona's good driving. She did a great job driving to and from Boston. He was very proud of her. And at the same time, he was relieved nothing happened since Fiona was a minor without a drivers' license. But he had to take chances. He wanted to see again and would do just about anything to make that happen.

Fiona drove like an old pro. All that practicing in the cemetery paid off. Tony always said that Fiona couldn't kill anyone there, because they're already dead. They had a unique friendship; he could be honest with her, and it was okay coming from him. Martha was a different story. Fiona felt as though she'd been driving forever, and in retrospect, he had.

The next appointment also went well, and Fiona drove again, and when they got home, they couldn't wait to tell Martha the good news. His left eye was healing wonderfully. He didn't need to wear the patch anymore. But to top it all off, Tony and the doctor scheduled surgery for his right eye now. He figured he had to do his part to get his sight back.

Tony ended up going through with the surgery. But that's the day Tony's life changed, and everyone's lives on the ride with him would change forever too.

When Tony woke up from surgery, he felt his eye with his hand, and there wasn't a patch like last time. He asked the doctor why.

The doctor told him, in a most professional way, that they ran into some complications that stopped them from doing the surgery. *That explains no patch,* Tony thought. He continued to inform Tony about being in the early stages of kidney failure. It crushed him. He felt so defeated before he could ever get a running start. *Could this be happening?* he asked himself. You bet your life it could! And it was! Then he was told that he had to stay in the hospital. They still needed to do a small surgery on his arm; basically, they had to retie some veins to the artery so that he could receive a special needle to have dialysis treatments. And they did this surgery while he was wide awake, starting with numbing the arm.

He became nauseous during the procedure just knowing what they had to do. But he had some distractions when it was over. They placed him in the hallway of the hospital at Mass General Hospital, all bandaged up. There were people on stretchers waiting their turns for a room, parked all along the walls of the hallways. Tony thought maybe they would put him on a stretcher to line up for a room. *But that's foolish,* he thought, when it's just his arm. But he doubted they would let him go home. They would have to watch out for infection, and diabetes, which had been out of control for years. This was all just coming to a head. Many days of feeling lousy have passed up until this point. And he had to face facts.

He couldn't help feeling like he had let Martha and the kids down. This was a man with dignity and ethics, pride and honor. He was an honest, hardworking man who worked three jobs when he had to. And now he was helpless, at the mercy of the system that should help him in his time of need. And the more he thought of it, the more it disgusted him and just made him feel worse. But this was a road already in progress, with no U-turns anywhere, one-way, full speed ahead, inevitably, and most probably, to a dead end. At least that's what Tony thought. But he was brought up with much faith in God and Jesus and the Holy Ghost. And he knew this was going to turn out however it was supposed to. He had already suffered intensely for some years. Besides, how bad could it really get? He always looked at everything positively, so he had that going for him. He healed well after his short stay at Mass General Hospital. They had him straightened out and feeling better in no time. He was amazed and very grateful. The hospital staff had been so good to him and he always had them in stitches with his humor. The staff were going to miss him, but Tony was ready to go home.

His arm was healing, and he was scheduled for dialysis three days a week, and that would make him feel better, so they said. But after his first treatment of dialysis, he looked rather green. And weak. He became a permanent fixture on the couch, vomiting, feeling lousy.

The doctor decided to increase his visits to five days a week to see if that would help Tony feel better. And it did help him out at first. But as time went on, he had become weaker. It was apparent that he was not a good candidate for dialysis. He wouldn't live another year at this rate. The doctors suggested a kidney transplant. But Tony was so weak, he sure didn't jump up and down. But he was happy to know he had the option.

His brothers and sisters would be tested to see if there would be a match.

Tony had many siblings. The large family started in St. Samuel, Quebec, Canada. They lived on a farm, and everybody helped. They made their own soap and many other things.

They had many cows, and it was Tony's job as a child to round up the cows at the end of the day. He had help from his sheepdog, who would run behind each cow, nipping at the back of their legs, and then ducking. He would be a great help to steer them into the fenced pen, and Tony would put the latch and the pin on the gate. Voila! What a team.

Until one day, the dog got hit by a car. It was a surprise to both the dog and Tony, since neither had ever seen a car before. They didn't know what it was. This happened in the 1940s, but he never forgot it.

Tony was the eighth child of nine in all. He was the last boy. He had three brothers and five sisters. His mother had an unbreakable faith, and the old man enjoyed his booze. He always had a glow, and loved to cheat at cards.

Tony's parents had been gone for some time now, but he still had his siblings. And they were all living in the States, and every one of them wanted to be the kidney match to help Tony live. The whole family just assumed his sister Giselle (who had been a nun for years) would be the match. But to everyone's surprise, she was not.

She came in second to Tony's oldest sister Ollie, who never had any children and adopted a baby boy from Canada years before. So everyone was ecstatic that some-one was a kidney match. How wonderful! It was a very sure thing that his chances of not rejecting her kidney were good. Tony was never so happy. He laughed and cried and joked, and told his sister Giselle that she was his ace in the hole, with tears running down his cheeks. She laughed with him and told him she was ready.

Tony rested easy that night in his hospital bed know-ing there was still hope. He had all his faith in God. He always referred to God as "Big Louis," pronounced Lou-E.

Tony's nature was to joke about everything, and he always tried to protect his kids.

But Martha, poor Martha, she sure did her part in this department. She always ran a tight ship. But she felt herself losing her grip.

Tony's sisters gave Martha much comfort. They drove her to Boston and accompanied her when they visited Tony in the hospital. They all took turns driving Martha to Boston to allow Fiona to attend school. And they'd get to see their brother Tony.

After school, Fiona always took the train to North Station and walked to MGH, Mass General Hospital, and back again for three months until Tony came home. Fiona was in the ninth grade now, and high school needed to be taken seriously. She had missed so much school in the past. Of course, all the teachers and the principal knew what was going on with her father, Mr. Tony Disolets (pronounced Diz-o-let). Tony always found it peculiar how his name was so close to Martha's maiden name, Doucette (pronounced doo-set). The faculty tried to be gentle with Fiona, who was going through a lot, but these days Fiona wasn't getting much supervision, which left her itching for some fun.

When nobody was home, but the car was, she would take off in her parents' car, without a license yet, and go pick up a ton of friends. She had lots of friends—in every town, it seemed. There'd be arms and legs hanging out of every window. They'd all pile in. She always told her friends that if they could fit in the back, then they could come, and she would drive everyone to a place called High Tower, a party place by the power lines. It had a beautiful view of the city below. Everyone smoked pot and drank Boone's Farm and beer. And it never failed; someone would show up with the hard stuff, the devil's brew. There was always a bunch of cars, and a great big bonfire in the middle of the sandpit everyone was parked in. Car radios blaring, garbling every word sung.

And Fiona always found out where the next party would be. And the next one, and the next one, and so it went on. It went on for a long time before anyone noticed.

Even after Tony came home from the hospital, Martha would get picked up by her sister Michelle, and they'd be off to bingo till 11 p.m. Tony was always passed out on the couch, and so Fiona would sneak off with the station wagon and pick up the gang and go party on. Fiona had always been sheltered from all the pain the real world had to offer. Her brothers were a bit older than her and to them she was the baby. And the matters that concerned them certainly didn't need a babysitter's opinion. But that all changed when Fiona hit puberty. She was becoming very independent in her early road to womanhood.

She was a godsend to Tony though. She was a nurse to him. He even told her she should become a nurse (she'd grown up in hospitals, giving her much practice). And all those trips to Boston's Mass General Hospital. All those laser treatments he had been through, even through snowstorms, and then not being able to fix the other eye, because of all things, his kidneys were failing.

As for Martha, the walls were closing in around her. She kept thinking, *When will it end? First I lose my precious baby, and now my husband may die at an early age?*

She wasn't coping very well. She prayed to God to keep her strong. She gave him all her cares. Her faith was solid. She was needing a little space and distraction from all these issues that kept following her and her family; she needed an escape. And her escape was running off to bingo during the week, running from problems. Fiona took after her in this aspect.

Martha would leave Fiona to tend to Tony's needs. But once he was out like a light, he would sleep for hours, and Fiona would sneak out to her party world for escape herself. There was *always* someone waiting to join her. She would get very buzzed, as buzzed as she could get by 11 p.m. She'd sneak into her bed, always beating her mother home. She'd parked the car in the exact same spot every time so Martha wouldn't notice. Martha had no idea.

There was the one time though, Martha was suspicious, but she had enough going on, and on her plate at this point, so she just let it go. *Pick your battles, do not look for any more problems.*

But as time went on, Martha began noticing a big difference in Fiona. Some big changes. She was dating and coming home all hours of the night. And if she didn't feel like it, she wouldn't come home at all. To Tony and Martha, this was not okay. Fiona had managed to become Miss Very Independent in the absence of, well, the entire family quite frankly.

# Chapter 5

When Fiona returned home from Boston, she had little time to get ready for a cookout that she was invited to from a friend from school. A bunch of them were meeting to go together. It was just another routine party for Fiona, but this party would turn out to change the course of her life. Fiona had no idea who the person was that was actually throwing the party, but that never stopped her or her teen friends, the party group, and Fiona always took the station wagon to make it possible to fit anyone who wanted to go.

The bunch of them arrived at the party site, which was hidden in the woods a little ways. They had a mild scuffle over who had to carry the cooler, but they voted the lasts ones in could do it. They all followed the path that led them right to the bonfire. The fire was roaring and reaching about fifteen feet or so. It was crackling and looked like it was dancing to the music that was blasting out of the radio or boom box at full volume. There were minors everywhere and everyone was drinking alcohol. Another fun time.

Fiona was mesmerized by the fire, but she just happened to look over it and noticed a boy who was watching her every move. Their eyes met, and for her it was love at first sight. She had never felt anything like it before. Something came over her as she knew she had to have him.

His eyes were beautiful to her—a deep dark brown that could stop anyone in their tracks. He was very good-looking and had that tough look she liked with huge muscles. She could tell just by looking at him that nobody gave him a hard time, if they knew what was good for them. It didn't take long before the two of them worked their way around the massive fire until they stood face to face and just began talking. He took care of himself, she admired him for that, being so young and already on his own and everything. Turns out he was a toughie. He had spent years bouncing in and out of foster homes. He was a runaway with no specific place to call home, and Fiona felt bad for him and wanted to fix it all and do whatever she could and help him in any way. The poor kid had been japed for having decent parents, and Fiona just so happened to be taking a course in psychology; therefore, she could fix everything. So they ended up dating exclusively. She became obsessed with trying to make life perfect for him. She loved him and wanted to make him happy. She knew it was love because before this guy (Mickey Melouin was his name), she dated many boys and ditched many, and it didn't even matter or faze her in any way. She tossed them out like trash and never gave it another thought. She was a player. Guys had little value to her, and she became a player without realizing it. And she never looked back when she was done with someone, never looked them up again. Done meant done.

Unknowingly, Fiona broke a lot of hearts. It never fazed her in the least. But this one she had to have and keep. And she had won him over.

It was so easy for her; she was vibrant and beautiful, and pleasing to the eye, with her long dirty-blond hair and big blue eyes and tiny dancer physique. And she was funny, always had a quick comeback for virtually everything, making everyone laugh with her contagious laugh inherited from her father. She was funny and everyone loved to be around her. And so did Mickey.

It turned out that he was supposed to leave that party with some tough chick Janice. But he had left with Fiona that day. And the rest was history.

Fiona fell deep in love with him as their relationship progressed. Mickey always made her feel so loved. She knew she wanted to be with him. He would always look right into her eyes as he'd hold her in his arms and give her the look of love before he'd attempt to jump all over her. And she melted like wax every time.

Fiona felt as though she were grown up, which was something she'd always fought for: her independence. She wanted to be all grown up so bad. But she was, in fact, very vulnerable and easily influenced, and very naive. But in her own mind, she was ready to take on the world. It just so happened that she and her boyfriend were inseparable. She would stay overnight with him and Martha would get furious. She wouldn't stand for this lying down. Every time Martha and Fiona discussed it, they would get into a fight and argue. Martha told her to wait until she was done with high school to move out and sleep over at Mickey's place. But Fiona abhorred Martha whenever she tried to tell her what to do. Fiona had become a wise little shit and broken her mother's heart. But she continued to sleep over at Mickey's place just the same. That night, as Fiona lay in bed, she shouted, "Fuck you mom and fuck your God, I'll do whatever I want. I'll get pregnant and drop out of school if I want! Nobody tells me what to do!" But little did she realize at the same time that as she blurted those words out, she was damning God and cursing her life. A pebble tossed into a calm and peaceful pond of life causes ripple after ripple, but Fiona tossed a boulder, causing tsunami waves.

Martha spoke to Mickey alone one day without Fiona knowing about it. She plead with him to talk some sense into Fiona, and talk her into going back to school before it's too late, and to come home till school ends. He did what he was asked, and it worked like a charm. Fiona was under his spell pretty bad and would do just about anything he asked her to. Everything worked itself out after the right decision was finally made, but those words Fiona blurted out would haunt her forever throughout her life.

One pebble tossed in still waters causes ripples all right! Fiona came back home, and just in time for Tony's return from the hospital.

Tony's kidney transplant was a success and things were beginning to look up. Fiona was under control for a while. His homecoming was emotional for all involved. The trip home from Mass General Hospital in Boston wore Tony out. He was exhausted. As soon as he sat in his recliner, he dozed off like a baby. He was so relieved it was all over, and he was back home in his castle. And Fiona had her buddy back and she was ready, willing, and able to care for him. In her mind, there wasn't enough she could do for him.

She stood up from the couch quietly so as to not wake her father. As she tiptoed out of the living room and into the kitchen, she approached Martha chain-smoking like a chimney at the kitchen table and offered to do the dishes. Martha didn't stop her.

"Fiona," Martha began, "I know you're good at taking care of Dad and even giving him his insulin when he cannot do it.

"Yeah," Fiona stated, "What are you getting at, Mom?"

"Well, Dad has a hole in his side with wicks sticking out of it and tubes going into it. The hole needs to be flushed out with a syringe a few times a day every day. You know I can't go near that kind of stuff, so if you don't want to do it, and you don't have to, a nurse will come every day to do it.

"That won't be necessary, I can handle it without a doubt," Fiona replied, putting Martha at ease.

"But you have to be reliable and be around every single day, Fiona. We can't always be looking for you," Martha said.

"How long does it have to be done?" Fiona asked her mother.

"I'm not sure yet. He goes to the doctor again in two days and we will know then." And without hesitation, Fiona told Martha to not pay for a nurse because she would be happy to help Tony out. She stayed home with good reason. Time passed on as Fiona stood by her father day and night and never left his side until she'd done everything for him that she was supposed to do. His kidney transplant was a huge success and it truly was a miracle.

# Chapter 6

FIONA DRIFTED FROM HER FAMILY. She couldn't care less if she didn't graduate. To her it was just a waste of time at this point. She had her head in the clouds. She was in love and ready to be on her own, with her own place and a job. She wanted desperately to be grown up and not need anyone anymore. But her judgment was lacking and she began to make bad choices. It seemed as though she didn't care about anything! It was hard to believe. This young girl who never shut up about having a sister, telling everyone who would listen, carried the loss around with her, feeling the weight of it. Underneath this "I don't give a shit" attitude she was screaming on the inside. It seemed as though life came to a halt. No more camping trips or vacations anywhere. In fact, Tony was selling the camper knowing those days were gone. And if they ever do come back, it won't be for some time. He had a hill to climb and it was going to be a rough road, although he had no choice. If he didn't give a kidney transplant a try, he was a dead man anyway. He figured he had nothing to lose. As far as Fiona went, she was depressed; she just didn't know it.

She was full of anger that this even happened to her father. He had been such a strong figure in her life, it was difficult for her to see him so sick. Fiona couldn't deal with it too well. She couldn't talk to her buddy Tommy because he was always at work. And Donny was two hours away at college. And she sure as shit couldn't talk to her mother about it because every time she tried, Martha would get all broken up about it. So Fiona didn't ask any more questions because she didn't want her mother getting all upset all over again.

The pressure of not knowing if Tony was going to live or die was too much pressure and too heavy a weight on both their shoulders. They both felt alone even though they had each other. Martha wanted to protect Fiona from the truth, but Fiona was no fool. She knew exactly what was going on. And she couldn't cope with this reality without help.

Slowly, almost innocently, she turned to drugs. The opportunity crossed her path at the right times—the wrong time really. Her friends wanted to "help her out." She was deep down in the dumps and the last party at High Towers was when she took her first hit of marijuana. She had felt a heavy burden lift right off her shoulders and it felt good. It had been a long time since she felt this good, this happy, so now she'd found her new escape. But this new friend (pot), waited for her at the entrance of a very wide and dark road that led to nowhere. Fiona never thought of consequences at hand; she couldn't see the end of the road, or the cause and effect, the dominoes of life. These were all too far down the road for her to worry about that now. But as she started down this ugly road, she experimented with many different drugs further along the way. Her sweet innocence was about to disappear, and that's when things got ugly.

Fiona thought she was pretty cool and that this would go unnoticed. But it didn't go unnoticed for long. Martha confronted her one day about it, how she quit dancing and changed friends and habits. But the more Martha tried to talk to her about it, the more rebellious Fiona became. She just wanted to be left alone.

"Don't worry about me, worry about Dad!" she barked back at Martha sarcastically. Martha's blood began to boil.

"Now you listen to me, I am worried about Dad. But I'm also worried about you. I'm your mother, you're my daughter, and I worry about you too, you know."

"Yeah, well don't bother," Fiona yelled back at her mother, slamming the bedroom door with the telephone cord crushed in the door and she tied up the phone for some time. She was planning her night (the great escape), with her new so-called friends. So she thought. They were excited to have another lost soul to drag down the dumps with them, deep into the trenches, through the quagmires, into the darkness. Fiona didn't realize that her book of life's pages were about to turn quickly as though a strong wind in a storm blew in and turned life's pages drastically. No U-turns. She became ugly, shall we say. Worst attitude. She cared about nothing. She was just an empty shell. And no matter what her mother had to say, Fiona didn't want to hear it. To Fiona, her mother was becoming the enemy always trying to stop Fiona from having her fun. She roamed the streets and hung out with other troubled kids at a street comer hangout with a stone wall in front of who-knows-who's house. And Martha hated for anyone to see her there with those bad influences. She drove up to them one time when they were all there hanging out and got out of the car and walked over to Fiona and grabbed her by a good handful of hair and forced her in the car and took her home. Martha was pumped. Fiona got grounded and everything. She lost telephone privileges—unheard of up until now. No cell phones. Fiona was livid. She was brewing and roaring with anger and just to show Martha who was boss and that she wasn't the one in control or going to get the last word, Fiona snuck out of her bedroom window and returned to the hangout laughing with her friends. It wasn't as though she felt like going back; she just did it to show her mom up. Here we go again with Fiona doing the opposite.

"To hell with her if she thinks she' going to tell me I can't do something! I'll decide!" Then she talked them all into moving the gang to somewhere else. She knew it was only a matter of time before her mother would be back for her, and she had no doubt that her mother would be much angrier with her for sneaking out. So they all walked to another party spot. She remembered she and Tommy used to go there to catch frogs together at the brook behind Sears Town Mall. Someone had brought shopping carts there and had them lying in the brook so you could cross the brook. Fiona and her friends hung out a while when she could hear her brother in the distance yelling for her as he was sent to search and find her.

"Over here, Tommy!" she shouted. "I can't hide from you and let *you* worry."

"Fiona," Tom replied, winded from climbing the hill to meet her, "you got to come home now."

"Fuck her, I am not going home," she said, pissed. But her brother knew how to talk to her and he really did handle her with TLC. They had always been very close, and if anyone was going to get through to her, it would be him. He began to tell her that he knew how she felt.

"Fiona," Tommy said gently, "you've made your point. It's undeniable. Mom knows how you feel, but she's so shook up about Dad. She doesn't need to worry about where you are all the time. I know you're upset about Dad too, but don't take it out on Mom anymore. Can you do that? For me?"

"Only because it's you asking," she said.

"Bye, you guys, I'm going to hit the road, I'll catch up with you another time." And she left singing, "Hit the road jack, and don't come back no more, no more…" And the crowd shouted back to her that they were out of there too. And they continued wishing her luck and telling her to stop being such a hard-ass. Then they threw dirt on the fire and put it out. Fiona and Tom slowly climbed back up the hill on a narrow path which led to the top of the hill where their neighborhood started. They walked home together as buddies, like they were since they were little. Tommy wanted to talk to her about his own problems that he knew Martha and Tony were not going to like.

"Fee," he said gently, "try to be easy on Mom. She's got her own problems. You got her freaking out."

"Good, she deserves it," Fiona said.

"I know you're just talking out of anger—no, I'm serious, Fee. Take it easy on her, will you? Please? Because I'm going to have to tell her that I met someone and got her pregnant," he told her.

"Cut the shit! Wow, oh boy, Mom's going to love that one! Good timing, bro! Ha, ha, at least I know that I'll be off the hook for a little while. Good distraction! Way to go, bro, congratulations!" They high-fived and then he put his arm around his sister as they walked home. When they got home, Fiona went straight to her room and didn't even look at her mother. She was giggling on the inside about her brother's news and knew Mom was about to get hit with another big wave in the rough seas she was already sinking in when she should've been sailing. And Fiona began to see the light and felt sorry for her mother. A lot was happening all at once, and it was overwhelming for everyone. It was one thing after another coming toward you a hundred miles an hour, like a runaway freight train out of control with its broken headlight and horn. Fiona began to feel very vulnerable to life itself. It was all very complicated and she was exhausted and sick of thinking about any of it. So she shut the bedroom light and went to bed worrying about her father, her best friend, her buddy.

The next morning Fiona was up early. She didn't get much sleep. Little catnaps here and there. She was feeling considerate for a change and left her mother a note that said *Gone to spend the day with Dad.* It was a Saturday morning and she walked to the train station which wasn't too far and purchased a ticket to North Station. From there she walked to the hospital. It was very crowded in the parking lot and at the entrance, and in the halls that led to the elevators. Everybody was in a hurry and just trying to get through the crowds. She squirmed her way through to squeeze into the elevator at the last minute as the doors closed behind her. There was a man looking at her, waiting for her to tell him which floor she was going to.

"Number eight please," she told him. The elevator moved so fast that when it stopped, she could feel her feet briefly come up off the floor. The number 8 lit up above the door as they opened and she exited. She knew that the hospital room doors that faced her had John Wayne in there. He had one of those great big rooms all to himself. Fiona couldn't believe he was in there a few doors down from her dad. As she entered her father's hospital room, the nurses were tending to him and they were just about done. Fiona sat down in a chair at the foot of his bed and waved to him with a big smile.

"Hi, Dad!" she said, still smiling.

"Hi, you're not by yourself, are you?" Tony asked.

"Yes, I am," she replied.

"What day is it?" he asked.

"It's Saturday, September first, 1979," she told him. The nurses were through and left the room as Fiona jumped up and out of her chair to give him a great big hug and kiss. His mustache had ice on it from his oxygen mask but she didn't care. He looked so weak. But it wouldn't be much longer for his kidney transplant. It was already scheduled and his sister Ollivette had to be admitted two days before to prepare her to be the donor. And Tony was being prepped so his body wouldn't reject the foreign kidney. It was serious, a matter of life and death. It wasn't sophisticated modem medicine in these days like we know it today.

Tony dozed off but Fiona didn't care. She just wanted to be with him so he wouldn't feel like he was going through this all alone. She was so attached to him, she was brave for his sake. She pulled the chair over to be next to Tony and dozed off herself. She dreamt about school and how much she had missed and how she was so far from learning anything. She couldn't concentrate to learn. Maybe after her dad has his surgery, then everything can get back to normal. Her dreams shifted over to her mother. She could see Martha standing there crying, nothing more. She awoke to the sound of someone knocking on the door. It was a woman with a food tray.

"Hi," Fiona said as she sat up.

"Good morning," the woman replied, smiling as she set the food tray down.

"I'll wake him in a couple of minutes."

The woman replied "Okay" as she left the room. Fiona bent over the bed rail to whisper into her father's ear.

"Dad, it's Fiona. I've got some coffee and does it smell good. And some toast." Tony's eyes opened and he smiled. Fiona grabbed the bed remote and positioned his bed as he began to slowly sit up. It was obvious how weak he was, so Fiona got everything ready for him. A little milk in his coffee just the way he liked it. And buttered toast. And chicken broth. Tony heard his stomach growling and forced the toast down with his coffee. As he talked with his daughter, his face had a happy glow; he always enjoyed their time together as much as Fiona did. They were alike and very close. Two peas in a pod. The day flew by like a breeze. Fiona didn't ever want to leave his side, but if she didn't leave now, there wouldn't be another train home until tomorrow. As they hugged and kissed each other goodbye, Fiona acted as though things were normal and there was nothing to be nervous about. She was always so strong for him. It just came naturally to her when it came to him.

"Too-da-loo, Dad," she said, "Get a good night sleep and I'll see you soon. I love you."

"Okay, Fee, I love you too," Tony said as Fiona disappeared from his sight. All he could think of was how young she still was and what if he didn't make it through surgery or if the new kidney transplant fails, or it rejects! She was too young to lose her father, he thought. He tried to stay positive as he tried to fall back asleep. But Tony worried about Fiona, and Tommy, and Donny in college. And he worried about Martha. She was so emotional these days. Overwhelmed. He could see his wife's face when he closed his eyes and fell asleep. He didn't know yet that he was going to become a grandfather. Fiona made it home safely. The trip back and forth to Boston had become routine to her. Martha was sitting at the kitchen table when Fiona walked in.

"Hi, Mom. Did you get my note?" Fiona reminded Martha how courteous she was for leaving her a note for once.

"Yes, Fiona, I got your note, thank you," Martha replied. "How was dad today?" she asked.

"He was real good, tired and weak, but he did well. He has a positive attitude and he keeps telling me that it'll all work out and not to worry."

"Sounds like your father," Martha replied, "but I bet he wasn't cracking any jokes."

"No, Ma, he wasn't. But he will again," Fiona answered her mother. "Just believe."

And then Fiona took one good look at her mother and realized she was terribly troubled about something. A light bulb suddenly went off in Fiona's head about Tommy's news of expecting a baby. She almost forgot all about it until just now.

"Mom, what is it?" Fiona asked. "Can I help?"

"Not now, Fiona, I've had enough for one day. We'll talk tomorrow, okay?" Martha asked as her eyes welled up with tears.

"Okay, Mom, tomorrow then. Good night." And Fiona walked over to where her mother was sitting at the kitchen table, chain-smoking, and from behind she kissed her mom on the head as she squeezed her shoulders as if to hug her. The kiss on the head reminded Martha of earlier days in Tori's crib with Tommy jumping and kissing her head. "We'll get through all of it, Mom, stay strong. It's going to be okay." And Fiona went to her bedroom and got ready for bed. Fiona knew Tom told her the news, she could tell just by looking at her. But she couldn't tell her mother that she already knew. She'd let her mother tell her in the morning and then she would have to act surprised. And when the time came the next morning, that's exactly how it happened. When Martha told Fiona, she was running out the door to catch the train to go see her dear ole dad.

"Mom, everything happens for a reason. This is a good thing, happy news, don't forget!"

"I know, you're right," Martha replied as Fiona ran out the door. An hour later, Martha's sister Michelle was outside in her car waiting to pick her up and accompany her to Boston to go see Tony. On the train ride, Fiona thought that was quite a turnaround for her mother and left it at that.

# Chapter 7

THE CHRISTMAS OF 1979 SNUCK up on everyone. Fiona still had her boyfriend and he was her first love. She really was in love with him. And she was certain he was deeply in love with her as well when he surprised her with a pre-engagement ring for Christmas. It surprised her parents too, as their mouths hung wide open. Martha knew better than to object unless she wanted to see her daughter flee. They both pretended to be happy for her. But he was not what they wanted for their daughter. He had nothing to offer her except a hard life. Martha prayed day and night for Mickey and his influence on Fiona to end. And she had unbreakable faith and knew it would only be a matter of time for God to work his powers.

The New Year rolled in like a wave ready to crash against the rocky shores. Tony was on tons of meds, but he was feeling good and back to a full recovery, although his blindness held him back. He wasn't completely blind, but he couldn't drive. He always described his vision as shadows in the light. He felt as though that good-for-nothing boyfriend of his daughter's was a shadow hovering over her beaming bright light that she had to offer the world. Martha's prayers were beginning to get answered. The punk hadn't come around for over a week now. Martha and Tony were just waiting it out to see what would happen now. And Martha had her fingers crossed, and was as always hoping for the best. Fiona had been brainwashed by this guy in thinking that he was in love with her. She never suspected a thing. She was 100 percent trusting of him, and never asked questions, figuring that he must love her completely and exclusively if he gave her a ring. And when she finally received a phone call from him, they went on and on like nothing ever happened, even though many days had gone by without hearing from him.

She was as blind as a bat! Never in a million years would Fiona have thought that he could ever step out of their relationship. But he did, and worst of all, she had to hear it from her friend Sequoia, who was just a tag-along friend. Fiona was devastated. She couldn't believe it.

"There's just no way he would ever do this," she told her friend Sequoia. But when Sequoia reminded her of that week when he fell off the face of the earth, Fiona's heart fell to her feet—her first heartbreak. In her heart, she believed that she couldn't live without him. And she never let him go.

She pushed her emotions right down her own throat and settled down about it to keep him. It ate her alive, like pouring grapefruit juice on an ulcer. It just ate away at her every day. Where is he? Who is he with? What is he up to? Is he telling me truths or lies?

He really broke a precious love that could've been his. He broke all the trust. He had it made. She never asked questions before, maybe looking back, she should have. Maybe she gave him too much freedom. It had to be her fault after all. But even so, things were never the same.

After Fiona got past the devastation, she became angry about Mickey's slipup. He pleaded with her that it would never happen again. He even cried for her entertainment. So she fell for it again. And again.

He started playing games with her. Slapping her around here and there, and controlling her. She would put lots of blue eye shadow on to cover up the bruises. She even covered up for him! In Fiona's mind, she needed him, had to have him, no matter what. Couldn't live without him. Loved him. He'd called regularly in the past, but now he was unpredictable. He didn't call when he said he would.

Fiona's gut churned inside her being, trying to tell her something was wrong. But when she saw Mickey that night, he confirmed all of her worst fears. When he arrived, as he shut off the motor of his 1970 Chevelle, he hesitated to get out of the car. When he finally opened the door and stepped out onto Fiona's driveway, he slammed the car door as he tried to look Fiona in the eye. He made his way to her standing there on the front porch, waiting anxiously to see him.

He sat down on the top step so she sat down beside him.

"Hi," she said to him. "Where's my kiss?" So he gave her a quick peck on her forehead. "What's wrong?" she asked as her raspy voice became deeper. "I can always tell when something's wrong," she stated as her voice began to quiver.

"Fiona, I am just stopping by for a few minutes because I have to tell you that we can't see each other anymore."

"But why? I thought we were fine?" He grabbed a hold of her and looked right into those sky blue eyes and told her that they were through.

"I'm not understanding this," she mumbled in disbelief. He's the one who gave her a ring, she thought. That meant that he wanted to be with her. She was confused. So she asked him again, "Why? I haven't done anything wrong and I've forgiven you."

"No, Fee, you didn't do anything wrong. But when I cheated on you, I got her pregnant. And we're getting a place together. So I can't see you anymore."

"Oh, you mean you would never cheat on her with me, but you'll cheat on me with her!" Fiona's blood was boiling. It got uncomfortably quiet. "You don't have to be with her just because you got her pregnant. It was an accident. We can still be together and then you can see your kid whenever."

He shook his head no. "We're done. I am with her now."

"Get off my porch!" she screamed at him. "I never want to look at you again!

You have no idea what you had! It's your loss, not mine! And here's your cheesy crackerjack ring!" And she threw it at him. He picked it up off the driveway, got into his car, and drove off. And Fiona bawled her head off. She ran into the house, storming through the screen door as she intentionally slammed it behind her. She was crushed and went straight to her bedroom and took out her photo album and began ripping every picture of the two of them right down the middle. Then she jumped on her bed facedown into the pillow and cried herself to sleep. Fiona had put up walls because of this breakup and protected her heart from then on, not allowing any real love to penetrate. She would be scarred for life.

> Success is not final. Failure is not final It is
> the courage to continue that counts.
> —Winston Churchill

# *Chapter 8*

TONY AND FIONA WATCHED TELEVISION together while Martha ran off to bingo. Fiona wept while she asked her father for advice.

"Dad, how do I stop hurting? I can't take it anymore!"

"Fiona, all's I can tell you is time heals all wounds. It just takes time," Tony replied as his heart tugged at her.

"I had a feeling you'd say something like that."

"Fee, you'll be okay, it takes time." It took some time for Fiona to move on. Her heart ached for Mickey. She had been so misled, so betrayed. Deep down, her parents were thrilled to see the unsavory character gone for good. They just couldn't let Fiona see their true feelings about the whole thing. Tony never trusted him and wanted more for his daughter. Tony and Martha both knew that she could do better than that. But as time went on, Fiona's heart hardened. She didn't trust men anymore, and she protected her tender heart that was locked up in a prison cell deep within her soul. She thought that Tori was lucky to be spared from this miserable life and all the pain that goes with it. Then she thought how she herself was lucky to have the opportunity to live, and somehow Tori's memory gave Fiona strength to stand tall and start fresh. Start over. Tori's spirit was drawn to Fiona and she wanted to make life easier for her, as though Fiona's heartaches were reaching out to her. She was there in the midst of everything. Her spirit was alive, a familiar presence to Fiona. Fiona wasn't going to get hurt like that ever again.

She finally slowly started dating again, but spent most of her time partying with her friends, drinking and medicating to kill the pain, unknowingly burying feelings, or she'd hang out with her brother Tommy. Both of their lives were changing as they matured and grew into young adults. Tom and his girlfriend Felicia got an apartment and moved in together. Soon afterward, Felicia gave birth to a baby girl, Sophia Marie Disolets, and Fiona was always over at their place. Every day after school, Fiona would bring her books first, and then walk only one block away to Tommy's place. She loved babies, wanted a bunch of her own someday, could hardly wait.

It all sounded harmless to Martha at first, but then one unsavory character replaced the next.

As time went on, Fiona spent more time—most of her time—at her brother's place hanging out with his girlfriend Felicia more than being at home. Fiona was fifteen now, still very naive, and Tom's girlfriend Felicia just turned eighteen, going on thirty.

The two of them hit it off as friends. Only one problem: Felicia became a bad influence for Fiona, sending her on her way to Party Hardy Avenue, teaching her more than she needed to know. Fiona, being so naive to know of any harm, never knew what hit her.

But Martha saw a big change in Fiona, objecting left and right. Fiona didn't listen or care. She had gotten a bad attitude and became defiant and rebellious.

It didn't matter one way or the other what her mother thought. The fight for independence was still going strong. But Fiona's innocence changed the course of her life.

It looked like Martha's hopeful thoughts were broken, but she never lost faith. It was another pebble tossed into still waters, causing ripple after ripple after ripple. Martha was awestruck. She lost her little girl. Those days of innocence were gone. But Fiona did manage to graduate in 1982, and that was a great accomplishment in itself that once had almost been cancelled.

Fiona was a hard worker. She had gotten herself a job on an assembly line at a plastic factory, Tilton and Cook, when she was fifteen. And now, two and a half years later, she still had her full-time job. She made a good days' pay and thought that was all she'd need to live her life. She never realized that she chose the hard road college could've avoided.

She turned eighteen in July that same year and found herself a small apartment. Martha pleaded with her to stay home and save some money and stay home awhile. But this yearning for freedom was embedded in Fiona's being. And when Fiona put her mind to something, there wasn't anything stopping her. It was the first time Martha and Tony were together alone in the house in years.

Martha felt empty and defeated and useless, with nobody left to tend to. Tony would try to comfort Martha by telling her how lucky they were.

"Honey," Tony said, "at least she could leave the nest and learn how to fly. That's better than being stuck with her for thirty years, isn't it?"

"Yeah, you're right, but it still takes getting used to, don't it?"

"Absolutely, take your time." And he hugged her. Of course, Martha's intuition could not rest. She knew her daughter and knew her wild and wooly ways, giving her good reason to worry. She was afraid her daughter would stray from the path to the promised land. Martha's gut told her everything. She always knew when Fiona was partying all the time. She'd go weeks without calling home, not even to talk to her father, and Martha was right every time. This child of hers was giving her too many gray hairs. Fiona had been experimenting all right. She was living without rules. Just the way she liked it. But when Martha finally tracked her down, reaching her on the telephone of her friend's house, she laid a huge guilt trip on her that was too heavy for Fiona to bear and carry on her shoulders.

"Fiona, Dad and I miss you, and he's wondering why you haven't even called him to see how he's doing all this time?"

"I know, Ma, I've been meaning to. It's just that I've been busy and working overtime to make some extra money and pay some bills," she testified.

"I understand, believe me," Martha replied, "but can I tell him you'll be stopping?" Martha asked hesitantly, not wanting to rock the boat.

"Yeah, let's see. Today's Monday? Is it okay if I come by on Thursday after work?" Fiona asked Martha.

"Sounds good, I'll make something for supper. We'll see you by six o'clock?" Martha asked gingerly.

"See you then, Ma," Fiona said, "and say hi to Dad for me."

"I'll tell him. Bye, honey, I love you."

"Bye, Ma, I love you too." And they both hung up the phone.

Thursday night finally came, and Martha felt as though it were the longest week of her life. She always sensed when things weren't right. Her woman's intuition was usually right on the money. Martha paced the kitchen floor as she placed the dishes and the silverware on the table just so, and Tony had his feet up as he relaxed in his recliner trying to read the newspaper and yelling at the television as he tried to argue with the weatherman.

"She's here!" Martha shouted excitably. Tony said nothing, reaching over to the side table for a cigarette and lit it. Then he folded up the newspaper on his lap and put it on the side table and smoked his cigarette, waiting patiently to see his little girl.

Fiona had her radio blaring so loud in the car that it was heard before she pulled into the driveway. It was a relief to everyone to hear the silence when she shut the motor. As she got out of the car, the door made a big noise as it screamed for some grease and then slammed shut. Fiona threw her big black leather purse over her shoulder and switched hands to smoke her butt. She was a heavy smoker like Tony. And so young. She always wore heels and that was all anybody heard—every loud step till she finally entered the door. Her hair was dirty-blond and all teased out. It was the eighties and big hair was in. She wore plenty of makeup and a tiny T-shirt and jeans and clogs. She was lucky if she was a size 3. And her little body was that of a tiny dancer. All those lessons paid off, and then some—a beautiful posture and big boobs to boot.

"Hi, Ma," Fiona said, greeting her mother as she flung her oversized purse onto the kitchen table. "Where's Dad?"

"Right in the parlor," Martha answered her.

"Oh, there you are, Dad." Fiona bent down over Tony in his chair and gave him a kiss.

"Hi, Fiona, how are you doing?"

"I'm doing pretty good, working a lot and paying bills. I'm up to date on everything and I have food in my fridge, can you believe it?"

"Yeah, is your car insurance current and your sticker?" he asked her.

"Yes, Dad, I'm good," she answered, finalizing the conversation. She put her cigarette out in his ashtray that had its own wooden stand, right next to his butt end, and next to his chair she walked over to the couch and just plopped herself onto it and joined Tony in front of the television. A few minutes later, Martha yelled for them to come and eat. Supper was ready.

"Oh my god, does that smell good," Fiona admitted.

"Boy, you aren't kidding," Tony agreed. Martha smiled and stood back while they helped themselves. It was Martha's specialty, her mother Elise's recipe: chicken fresco stew with dumplings, and the secret ingredient from Canada called Seriate, a French word meaning sweet-savory.

They all sat together at the kitchen table like old times. They enjoyed a long overdue dinner together. They laughed together about how hot they were after eating the soup. Tony kept using his handkerchief to wipe the sweat off his forehead, temples, and brows. Then he left and went over to the corner counter where he took his insulin.

His diabetes was out of control these days. That's why they moved so close to the hospital. He had his share of ambulance rides due to his sugar getting too high or too low in some cases. He was very close to being in a coma at one point. But they gave him a shot into his ankle artery and he suddenly came to. When Tony awoke, he said, "I could've been dead and I wouldn't have even known it!"

While Tony took care of his meds, Martha looked Fiona over. She could see her glossy eyes, and her being spaced-out was obvious. Martha half-chuckled on the inside seeing how easy it was for Fiona to fool Tony. But Martha wasn't fooled. She knew Fiona was drinking and into drugs. And she had a feeling it wasn't just pot. But confronting Fiona head-on about these issues never got anybody anywhere except further from the truth and she'd leave. Martha had to do the only thing she knew how. She prayed. All the time. And she knew she would have to this time too. Tony returned to the table as Fiona asked if there was anything for dessert.

"Of course," Martha replied, "there's always room for Jell-O." The night went by so fast, it seemed over so quickly. Fiona had offered to help Martha clean up, but Martha insisted she would do it later. Martha tried to have a little talk with Fiona, pleading with her to take better care of herself, not so much partying all of the time. But Fiona wouldn't have it. She'd blow up at Martha every time she brought it up. There wasn't anything Fiona hated worse than her mother trying to tell her what to do. Martha was finally beginning to realize that Fiona always did the opposite. She proved it time and time again.

"Thanks for the supper, love you, got to go, maybe I'll stop by next week, we'll see," and she jumped in her car and drove off disappearing into the night. Somehow, somewhere, Martha was viewed as the opponent versus the ally. So Martha had approached Tony.

"Tony, what can we do about her? I know she's all messed up!"

"She's eighteen, that's what eighteen-year-olds do! At least she's normal!" he replied. Martha went upstairs to bed upset. She worried so much about Fiona, her baby, out there all alone in this big, bad, ugly world. She couldn't protect her. Martha threw her arms up over her head and put her nightgown on as she sobbed. She looked at herself in the mirror as she brushed her long dirty-blond hair. She wiped her tears and got into her bed. She laid there, clutching her rosary beads as she prayed herself to sleep, praying for Fiona's safety.

Fiona was loving being on her own. She worked every day and met with her friends every night. And every weekend was a party, carefree and happy without a care in the world.

Martha called her weekly to try and keep her grounded, and to let her know her father's condition. Fiona would pop in from time to time, but not nearly as much as she should've. But all in all, they were glad to see that their little birdie that left the nest did indeed know how to fly. But in more ways than one.

They'd hear stuff from the parents of the neighborhood kids who used to hang out with Fiona before she found a new crowd about how she drank every day and went out every night. And her doing drugs. And to Fiona, the male species was disposable. Trust was dead. She was a pretty girl and they flocked around her like pigeons being fed in the park. Her one love whom she was crazy about crushed her.

It was as though her emotions had gone numb. Fiona was just like a piece of hard candy with its hard shell, but the center was still soft. She would from now on protect that soft, tender center of hers, her heart. She just didn't realize it yet.

Years would go by before anyone could get to the soft center where the biggest heart ever had been hiding scared. Fiona had been scarred for life. She acted tough to protect herself from getting hurt again. But those blessed gifts of a warm heart were bursting to pour out of her. There was more good in her than bad, and it was God's will to prove it. If she would just stop fighting him. But Fiona never stopped long enough to even think about how God worked. She had no idea how to open the door to blessing after blessing just waiting to be unleashed to her. It was her own fears and stubbornness blocking the channels. She didn't need anybody. Not even the great "I am."

Fiona was glad to arrive at her apartment. She was tired from working all week at the plastic factory, Tilton and Cook. They made everything there from barrettes and headbands and everything in between. Fiona loved her job. The assembly line and packing department was fast. They would speed up the conveyor belt and try to break their own time record and see just how much product they could produce for the day.

That made the job fun. And at lunchbreak, she and her work friends would drive down the street every single day as they'd smoke a joint on the way and they'd all order a mixed drink, or two, or three. Usually Fiona ordered rum and Coke, because it looked like a soda in a glass, in case someone from work would pop in. But by the end of each day, she had herself a regular workout! All she needed now was to get something in her stomach, and relax for a few, and she'd be ready to paint the town red! Going out drinking every lunchbreak and every night was just what she did without any second-guessing. She would either go to someone's house or to the nightclubs to dance her heart out. The drinking was automatic. Fiona had her father's mind set on the matter.

"I never miss work because of drinking, so I will drink whatever I want!" Tony would say. That was her motto too in life: friends and parties, all fun and games. She was her own boss. Little Fiona with her raspy voice and quick joke or comeback. She hadn't been labeled class clown for nothing. She was the spitting image of her father.

When she was little, she would ask her father whom she looked like, her father or her mother? And he told her that she had his features and her mother's fixtures! Whenever Tony looked at Fiona, he could tell that behind those beautiful sky blue eyes was a restless mind continually in thought. Those wheels were always turning at full speed. But he also knew that he was Fiona's hero, idol, and best friend. She trusted him completely and would listen to anything he said. He always knew how to handle her. Gently. She always took his advice. She recognized him as the king of the castle, and she had total respect for him. Tony was born in Quebec, Canada, in 1932, and moved to the US when he was only eight years old. Tony was dignified and proud. Also a perfectionist.

Things had to be in their place. He was dark and handsome, with dark brown eyes and dark skin, most likely from his Indian roots. He had a deep voice and an awesome smile and a contagious laugh. Lots of spunk and humor. But illness always overshadowed his life. He showed lots of bravery in the hospital during all those visits and surgeries and mishaps.

When he was eighteen, he had to have his goiter taken out and he nearly died from losing too much blood. The doctor stopped the surgery immediately, Tony was losing too much blood and almost died. They would have to do the operation in two sessions. But, in the meantime, the cut across his neck wouldn't be allowed to heal until after the second surgery. When it began to heal, they had to peel the new skin off so it wouldn't close. It was held together with butterflies.

When he was twenty-eight, he became a bad diabetic. Back then, there was no such thing as disposable needles or syringes; Tony would have to boil them. He didn't even know he had diabetes until the day of his boss's party. Everyone thought he was just drunk and horsing around when he started rolling around on the front lawn. When they called Martha to come and pick him up and get him out of there, she took one look at him and said to call the ambulance. And that was the day Tony found out he was a diabetic. Tony had been doing pretty good since then, health-wise, until he started to lose his vision. Tony couldn't deal with it. He didn't take it well at all. But as soon as he got over that hump, he was facing an even bigger one: a kidney transplant.

But he was remarkable, he pulled through it with flying colors. The doctors put him in the medical history books. All Tony had to worry about was his body rejecting the kidney, which it never did. Thank God. Tony was one of the lucky ones when it came to that. Kidney transplants were not too common then in 1979, when Tony got his. So he never had it easy. But he was proud of his accomplishments. In the gentlest of approaches toward Fiona, touchy subjects were just that, and Martha left that up to Tony. He wanted to instill in his daughter values and honor, class and character, integrity and ethics, pride, all of it. And Tony was the only one Fiona would ever consider listening to, besides Tommy. But he always managed to sit her down long enough to engage in a real conversation. She had stopped by after work to see Tony, so he said what he had to say. "Fiona, you have got to slow down. If you get thrown out of your apartment for having too many parties, well, you're going to hate coming back home," Tony told her a gentle voice. And then he continued.

"And it won't be easy after being on your own to have to follow the rules at home. But if you do come back home, our rules will be followed. You do know that, right?"

"Oh, do I," Fiona replied unenthusiastically. "Oh, Mom will just love that," she stated. "I've got to go, Dad, but I'll stop by in a couple of days, all right, Dad?" Fiona asked.

"Sure," Tony said, "sounds good. Until then be careful, all right? Use your head. Try not to make your mother worry so much."

"That's impossible. Okay, give me a kiss, I'm out of here. Say hi to Mom. Bye, Dad, love you."

"Yup," Tony replied, "see you later." When Martha arrived home later that evening from bingo, she tiptoed through the house and went to her bedroom. She could see that Tony was sound asleep in his La-Z-Boy reclining chair and he was finally sleeping comfortably, and she didn't want to wake him. Later on during the night, he awoke in his chair and got up and joined his wife and went to bed. As he crawled into the bed and under the sheets, he could tell Martha was still somewhat awake, because he could hear her rosary beads rubbing together as she faithfully prayed for that wild daughter of theirs. Tony chuckled to himself thinking Martha's beads would wear down to just strings, like dental floss, being used so much by Martha. Then Tony rolled over to his good side and quickly fell back to sleep.

# Chapter 9

IT WAS ANOTHER MONDAY MORNING and the beginning of a new week. Fiona's employer became worried about her when she didn't show up for work. Fiona had a perfect attendance for her first year working there, and now she missed three Mondays in a row. When she showed up for work on Tuesday morning, her boss wanted to see her in his office.

"Good morning, Mr. Roberge," Fiona said to him politely.

"Good morning, Fiona. Come on in and shut the door behind you. Have a seat and we'll start in a few minutes. I'm just waiting for your supervisor, Allen, to join us for your review."

"Okay," Fiona replied. She wasn't the least bit nervous about being called to the office for a meeting with her higher-ups. In fact, she had a pretty good idea what this meeting was about. She knew she'd been missing a lot of work. She was a perfectionist like Tony; it bothered her too, not having a perfect attendance any longer was definitely a red flag. She barely had time to pull up a chair when the office door opened and Allen came walking through the door and into the office. He was such a nice supervisor. He was fair and realistic when it came to quantity and quotas, and with records to break and deadlines to meet. He was good to his help and everyone respected him for that. And he liked Fiona; she was always bubbly and funny and honest and kind. And Fiona looked up to him.

"Fiona," he said as he grabbed a chair and pulled it closer to her, "I'm worried about you, girl. Is everything all right? I want you to know that this conversation is completely confidential and neither I nor Mr. Roberge will ever repeat what is said in this office." And then he went on to say, "We care about you and we want you to be safe and we know something is wrong and, well, quite frankly, we want to help you in any way we can. Will you let us help you?" Fiona burst into tears. He had hit a nerve and got through to her, knocked down that wall.

"I'm very sorry, you guys," she said sobbingly as Allen handed her the tissue box.

"Fiona, forget the job," Allen said, "it's you we're worried about! Let us help you." Allen was most sincere and truly did want to help her. "Tell me what's been going on. I know you broke up with your boyfriend recently. Has he been hurting you?" Allen asked. She broke down again just hearing the truth out loud.

"Yes, Allen, you hit the nail right on the head. He's been coming by my apartment on the weekends ever since we broke up and yes, he has hit me a few times."

"I knew something had to have been happening to you, Fiona! You never miss work. And you've never come to work with makeup on since recently. Just another abrupt change I've seen in you."

"Well," Fiona said, "to be honest with you, I was try-ing to cover up the black-and-blues on my eye with blue eye shadow. He has handled me a few times and I was trying cover up for him, can you believe it?" This Mickey loser had been cheating on his new girlfriend with Fiona.

"Would you like some time off to sort things out?" Allen asked.

But she grabbed another tissue and wiped her eyes as she declined the offer. "Thank you very much for the offer; it's just that I can't afford to take any time off. I'll be fine and thank you for the pep talk. I really do appreciate your concern, I am embarrassed to say the least," she stated as she got up to leave the office and return to work.

"Nonsense, don't feel that way!" Mr. Roberge interjected as he stood up from his desk. "We're just looking out for you, Fiona," he said with authority. "You can talk to us any time you need to or want to."

"Thank you, Mr. Roberge, and thank you, Allen. You're both very kind, thanks again," she said as she pushed in her chair and walked out of the office, closing the door behind her, thinking why she had to love that stupid jerk. When she got back to the assembly line, everyone stared at her with their eyes wide open at each other, waiting for Fiona to tell them what the meeting was about. They wouldn't come right out and ask her, but it was too emotional and personal of a topic for her to talk about, so she looked at her coworkers who were interested in her business and said, "Well, I guess I won't be missing any more work." And she left it at that and got back to work. Nobody questioned her and that was that. Tony and Martha had no clue that

Mickey had been beating their little girl again. If Tony knew about it, he would've had him pinched by the cops. That's how Tony would've put it.

Fiona didn't visit her parents until most of the bruising healed. She knew what he was doing to her was wrong. She was protecting that lowlife of a boyfriend from her again without realizing it. She didn't want to live without him and if Tony knew, that would be the end.

Fiona knew how much her father loved her, and she remembered those times she was alone with him. They had gone to the drive-ins, on picnics, and they even made Christmas candles together one year in Tony's workshop in the basement. And then, once Fiona quit cheerleading and dancing lessons after eleven years, and had girl scouts and school days behind her, Fiona had become fired up on boys—one particular bad boy. And he became one unhealthy habit. And she knew it. As much as it broke Fiona's heart, she knew it had to be done. The only thing she could love now was the memory of how she thought it was going to be. Because it never could be—oh, she would use him!

When she got to her apartment after work, she skipped supper because she had no appetite. Instead, she took a nice hot shower and got into her nightgown. As she combed out her long dirty-blond hair, she tried to hold back the tears, but she could not. She got into her bed, reaching over to the nightstand to shut the lamp. She then pulled up the covers and over her and put her face in the pillow as she screamed, sobbed letting it all out, crying herself to sleep. Fiona awoke every hour or two throughout the night crying, knowing it was over. And besides, he had a baby with Fiona's friend Sequoia, the old tag-along friend everyone tried to ditch, the one who told her Mickey was cheating in the first place, never letting on that it was with her! When she heard this, she ended her rendezvous with Mickey, and closed that door forever, never going back. Clearly she needed better friends. Why not just a whole new start?

# *Chapter 10*

FIONA SUDDENLY QUIT HER JOB without notice. So not like her. She figured everybody at work knew her dirty little secret of being battered. And she was no longer comfortable working there knowing they knew everything. She was embarrassed. Of course, Martha was overjoyed that her daughter had to move back home. She could finally sleep at night. Martha and Tony had no idea why Fiona was coming back home, and they were afraid to ask. So they didn't.

"If Fiona wants to tell us why, then she will," Tony commented. They just took it as a blessing, and thanked God that she returned home safe. Fiona was happy to be home. She was fractured into many pieces, and needed to rest and mend. Her heart had been shattered like glass and now she was at the lowest of lows. Her first heartbreak, twice!

It didn't take Fiona too long to settle in. It was almost as though she'd never left home. But things were different this time. She showed an appreciation toward her parents for all they've done for her, including putting up with her. She had never expressed appreciation before. Her tough chick persona was showing its softer side.

She grew up a little from the whole experience. But she never really got over him. She had been so fooled into thinking that the feelings were mutual. But she became bitter toward men and just expecting them all to be the same. She would never let true, raw feelings come into play again. She wore a hard shell like a hard candy with a soft center. She was heartbroken, and it scarred her for life. But her battle scars paralyzed her with inner pain that she couldn't stand to deal with anymore.

Before long, she began not caring about much of anything, and the old habits started to slowly creep back into her life. She was partying and drinking and drugging. Fiona didn't care what happened to her. She just had to kill the pain. Little did she know it was the beginning of her own demise. One time she took off to party with some strangers she met while walking to Martin's, the variety store at the corner. Nobody knew what happened to her for three days! Martha was ready to crack, fearing the worst. She paced the floor waiting for her son Tom to return with some good news from searching the neighborhood looking for her. He knew some of her hangouts and felt confident he could find her before Martha had a nervous breakdown. Tony sat back helpless, trying not to show that he was worried. Martha cried and cried.

"What if she was raped or murdered?" she shouted, blowing her nose again.

"Come on now, Martha, don't think that way, Tommy will find her," Tony replied. "You know that! They're close, and he always knows where to look. It'll turn out fine, you'll see." Martha kept on sobbing as she wiped her face with the last tissue in the box, marching and storming into the bathroom closet for another box, slamming the door.

Tony rolled his eyes. He was worried and fearing the worst—only natural. But he wasn't going to tell Martha. Hours went by before Tom found Fiona hanging out with some dropouts with too much time on their hands. Even her own brother, her closest ally, was surprised to see that her social circle had changed. He didn't recall her ever mentioning it. Tommy didn't know one person there. And she always told him everything, feelings and all. At least she used to. He felt outnumbered when he found her with them and saw it in her eyes that she had bounced back once again into her self-destruction mode 101. He hadn't ever seen her like this before. She was all fucked-up! For the first time in Tom's life, he was actually worried about his sister. They were like best friends and he could feel her slipping away. Fiona was in no condition to be reasoned with.

"Oh, there you are, Fiona! I've been looking every-where for you! I was hoping to find you here," Tom stated, approaching Fiona.

"What's up, bro? Join the party with me and my new friends!" she replied with her eyes half-shut and slurring her words.

"Well, will you come over here and talk to me for a minute?" Tommy asked. "I'm done talking!" Fiona yelled. "I've had it!" Then she lit another joint.

"I know," Tom tried to soothe her, "I know, Fiona. But it's no party at home either. Mom's getting ready to call the police to look for you! So come home with me now, so Dad will feel better too. He's not strong. Please? For me?" Tom pleaded. She got up from the chair she was sitting in, as she hung out in whoever's backyard she was in, and grabbed her brother around the neck so he could help her walk. They embraced like the best friends that they were, and then Tommy thanked her.

"Thank you, sis." And Fiona had to get the last word. "You had to go throw the dad card, huh?"

"Yup," he answered her with a smile from ear to ear as the two of them stumbled home. When they walked into the house, Martha exhaled loudly with a sigh of relief, wanting to smother her daughter with loving hugs but knowing better. And Tony gave her a look of great disappointment, stating very bluntly and boldly, "You had everyone worried."

"I'm sorry, Dad, really," she answered him, looking down at the floor to avoid looking him in the eye. She hated disappointing her father. She headed upstairs to her bedroom feeling broken. Shattered. Her thoughts went back to the love she once knew, before her dreams and hopes were ruined. She expected guys to be like her brothers and her dad, not a mean bone in their bodies. Fiona lay there in her bed in the dark as she sobbed through the night off and on, falling asleep and waking up numerous times. Poor Fiona. Betrayal was something she had never considered. All she ever wanted was to love and be loved in return. But instead, she was used and abused and fooled. And she knew it all stemmed from the one love she trusted crushing her, putting all those eggs in one basket. And she paid dearly for it emotionally, scarred for life. It followed her her whole life. Her heart calloused. She was screaming on the inside and couldn't bear the pain anymore. That's when she started to use whatever she could find to kill the pain; she wasn't fussy. Slowly, her life would become a runaway train, heading for the end of the tracks.

It was now the '80s, and she was in luck. The greatest number of all times—cocaine—was everywhere! Time flew by for Fiona; of course, she was always speeding.

She weighed maybe a hundred pounds by now, and everyone was noticing. But she didn't care. She didn't feel anything anymore in fact. And that felt good to her. Finally she felt good.

As time marched on, it took its toll. Life became a party, a celebration of not feeling anything! No more wearing her heart on her sleeve! She was through with all that!

She did well as an employee, but once she clocked out at the job for the day, the party began. Her cooler was always full of ice and beers for the road—her reward system for working all day at minimum wage. Some nights spent clubbing, dancing, drinking, and drugging would turn into a house party somewhere, always turning into all night until morning! As long as Fiona had her so-called friends to do it with, she could pull off working all day after an entire night of partying. And before long, there was no space between, the party never ended. The day and night connected.

It became her lifestyle. Her life was a party, as she suppressed all those feelings even deeper, never dealing with them.

All her money went to either concert tickets or drugs or booze. And if a concert was out of state, don't think that stopped her from going! She would just add in the cost of gas, food, and lodging. Make it a vacation, why don't you? As long as she was high and partying, she was up for anything. She worked overtime for it.

Nothing ever stood in her way. When she faced an obstacle, she would find a way to go around it or over it. Just like all those suppressed emotions she would face and deal with, this lifestyle was how she got around them. What do you expect from an eighteen-year-old. This continued, though, for many more years of her life's journey as she began to spiral. And then, she slowly began to lose her grip on reality, becoming unfocused, lost, distant, empty, always expecting the other shoe to fall off, as the saying goes. She even stopped mentioning Tori to everybody she encountered. Fiona had always had a connection with Tori's spirit. It was a true gift of the psyche, and this made Tori's spirit helpless and restless, rejecting the separation. Tori's thoughts whispered in the heavens.

"If only I had lived and not died, maybe I could've helped my sister through these hard times, although if I lived, she might have not even been born. Or maybe she wouldn't have ever turned to drugs.

If I had lived, we would've been closer sisters, and I would've helped her. I hate to watch her suffer like this. She had so much light. I, Tori, would've been an older sister to Fiona, and I would've protected her. I've got to help her if I can. Even though I've passed on, there has got to be something I can do from here to help her though.

Although we have never met, she is my sister. She is a part of me, my baby sister. And she always kept my spirit alive.

I kneel and pray to the Almighty God, as my heart bleeds for her. I cannot watch her suffer any longer. Her pain becomes my pain, as though we are one. I live on through her.

I passed two years before Fiona was born. God took me and cradled me in his arms when I passed from a heart defect under two years old on February 13, 1962, declaring me an angel, just like Dad said. There were no cures or medicines for something like that in the 1960s.

My sister Fiona always made sure that people knew that I had once lived. She always included me like an imaginary friend. I was still a part of the family because of her. They stopped trying to forget me. And I've got to love her for that, and try to help her if I can. She may be able to tune everybody else out, but she can't tune me out, because I'm always with her. And I will call out to an army of angels if I have to.

I didn't get the chance to live for long, but she is still alive and I can't watch her destroy herself because of painful encounters; life is full of them. She is pushing her life down to the depths of death, mourning her life as though she is already dead.

May my tears, as a misty shower, fall down upon her like holy water that heals and comforts. Now it is different, she doesn't even know I'm here. But I have seen her whole life from the bleachers of heaven, rewarded as an angel, for dying as an infant. I live on through her. I cannot let her waste her life; I have got to help her somehow! I'll open my wings and soar straight into the arms of the Lord of hosts, the one true God and creator of all mankind. My urgency will be felt in his presence as his love and tenderness surround me. 'All is well,' he will say to me. And his love will see us both though these trials which are designed to bring us closer to him to get to know him."

# *Chapter 11*

IT WAS NOW THE END of August of 1982. Fiona was ready to move out and be on her own. She consoled Martha, telling her she did a good job if her little birdie has confidence to attempt to fly out of the nest in the first place.

"And I, Tori, wasn't going to stop keeping an angel eye on her. After all, she is my sister. And I'm also her guardian angel. In fact, all angels are everyone's guardian angel. I want her to enjoy the life she was so graciously given, especially because of mine being but so short. I can live through her keeping my memory alive. I once lived! And I could try to steer her from dangers that only I could foresee, with God's grace of course. But I could tell my sister Fiona was ready. She wanted so bad to be all grown up. What she didn't know was that it was going to be a lifelong process. She would have to adapt to and tackle obstacles, heartaches, and plain old life lessons. Oh the suffering, especially if you are one of his chosen ones. And I, Tori, will always do my best to direct her toward that sometimes lonely, yet everlastingly rewarding narrow road."

But Fiona's heart was severely scarred. Fiona was wan and disheveled. And she was vulnerable, looking anywhere for some relief for the symptoms that she felt. It wouldn't be long until the serious partying began. There's nothing wrong with having fun and enjoying friends and youth. But what started out as fun turned into an addiction for her. It wasn't just that she was the only one with an apartment for everyone to hang out at; she also had a mucilaginous personality that drew everyone to her. Eventually, Fiona grew tired of tripping over drunkards sprawled out on her living room floor, and told them all the party was over. She managed to pull the reins in for a while. It was time to set the meter.

"And since I, Tori, consider myself to be somewhat of a patrician, considering that I'm with the all-powerful, present, and knowing omnipotence, I'm confident he will support me in this endeavor with his legions of angels. His power will cause a roaring conflagration against those who are choosing to harm my precious sister, Fiona. It will be his winnowing strength, and only my assistance, that will become her only survival. For as time marched on, I saw Fiona repeating the same mistakes time and time again! And the biggest one of all was trusting the wrong people. But these infamous rebels won't know what hit them. There will come a day when their plight will not be contemptuously ignored. But for now, they continue to sell their indulgences. But God's supplest strengths shape and mold Fiona, for with him is her only hope. And eventually, her meekness will shine!"

Fiona's crowd of friends was fastidious and she loved to feel needed—a codependency among them all! Well, at least between her and Rachael Johnson and Sequoia Matthews. They were all guilty of forever carousing one another. And when they smoked too many drugs, they weren't fussy. Sequoia would think that she had some kind of power of divination.

"Any believer knows that the Lord despises this!" Tori cried from the heavens; Sequoia would realize this eventually, for it would become a major pitfall! And this storm of indignation would not go unnoticed! As for Fiona in her crucial state, the Lord will anguish her to himself in her supplication. And she will laud him with his ingenuity. He will smelt her with heat, and begin separating the good from the bad, in due time. I hope and pray!" Then Tori's spirit dissipated like the morning dew.

# *Chapter 12*

PRESENTLY, FIONA WAS BORED WITH life. Get up, go to work, come home, and party. Day after day! She thought the same old things! She was ready for a change. There just had to be more to life than this!

She concocted this convoluted idea to drive across the country and maybe settle down in California or New Mexico or Arizona, or even Las Vegas! She would have to see. But she knew her mother would freak out on her. So she would break it to her father first, in the hopes that he would understand. And he did, when she finally got her nerve up to do so. And how did he react? His exact words were "I'm surprised it took you this long!" So, with that said, it pretty much gave Fiona his confirmation. But he did say, "You're not going alone!" And she did agree. So for now, her mission was to seek out a partner in crime, so to speak, someone else ready for adventure! She thought of Sequoia Matthews. But she wouldn't be able to. And they weren't close friends. And she stated outright, she's got a kid now, by Mickey! So that idea was out, but maybe Rachael Johnson would jump on it! *She's in the same boat I'm in!* Fiona thought to herself. *All she does is get up, go to work, come home, and party! Maybe she would enjoy this adventure!* And sure enough, when Fiona called Rachael, she jumped all over the idea!

Rachael's parents were divorced, and life was very different. Her dad was long gone, and her mother had a new life. And Rachael was always left alone anyways. So she was more than ready.

They called each other back and forth all week in preparation for their journey to begin. Both girls gave their jobs no notice. Neither planned to return. But avoid that subject at all costs they did. Martha was fuming! She didn't like the idea at that! She wanted things to stay simple and safe and unchanged.

"What if you run into some kind of trouble?!" Martha pleaded with tears in her eyes and running down her cheeks and a frog in her throat. "Huh, Fiona?" You see, Martha knew that changed circumstances would trigger a cavalcade of problems. And all Martha could think was these girls had gumption, right? It's not like either one of them had a tumultuous childhood. So why did she have to worry about them becoming ominous denizens of death! Because Martha knew Fiona like a mother is supposed to know her daughter. And she knew Fiona's heart was terribly scarred and forever affected by the betrayal she endured right out of the gate! And her track record so far showed Martha that she had good reason to worry, because Fiona always turned to drugs and alcohol to numb the pain of life's scars, instead of dealing with it appropriately.

Then Martha remembered seeing all the males around her daughter with their salacious manners. And that's what worried her! *We can't help her if she's thousands of miles away!*

she thought. And so Martha worried and worried. She knew there wasn't anything that she could do to stop her, and that was a painful reality for Martha. Sometimes the truth hurts.

All the monsters of Martha's own mind were ganging up on her with all the possibilities of what could happen to her beloved Fiona. She couldn't bear losing another daughter. So many what-ifs.

She collected herself in a timely fashion and prayed to God for more faith in his miracles. And it started to look like that's what it was going to take for Fiona's spirit to be content. Let it go! Hopes and dreams are great, but not if these make you lose your present, the right now of life! Life—forever renewing and improving, and rebuilding new hopes and dreams.

"Don't get stuck, Fiona! I wish you could hear me!" Tori cried from heaven's abyss. "And Mom too for that matter! Wish you could hear me, Mom! I know you're worried and feel the same way that I do!" And Tori vanished into the background of time, as though the blinds of heaven's windows opened but were busy all the while on Fiona's behalf, toiling in the spirit world. Martha trusted in the Lord alone that his will be done. It was hard for her knowing she might lose Fiona. She knew it was a strong possibility.

But hopefully it would not last. It pained Martha just knowing that Fiona would face trials.

# *Chapter 13*

Tori's spirit became restless. She whispered in the heavens.

"I now know that my purpose in my spirit life is to be Fiona's guardian angel. And I can see why God made it this way, because Fiona faced danger at every comer, all day, every day. If I don't intervene and stay with her, she would surely meet her premature demise. And my purpose in this universe is to assist God in keeping her safe."

Fiona had been driving for hours and the road became mesmerizing. She kept on blinking her eyes, trying to shake it off. Finally, she told Rachael that she was pulling the car over at the next exit to gas up and get a drink, and use the restrooms. At this point, they were in Arkansas, and the longer they drove, the more it all looked the same, like a boring slideshow. Another half hour passed before they saw any exit, but once they did, they were relieved, especially since the low gaslight had been on for a while. Fiona pulled the car up to the gas pump. As she got out of the car, Rachael did the same. They walked into the store together and headed straight for the munchies. Fiona bought some almonds and an iced coffee. She also paid the man at the register thirty dollars for gas on pump two. Rachael bought a pink lemonade and gummy bears. They walked out together, Fiona pumped the gas, while Rachael had the key to the restroom. When she came out, Fiona went too. Later, they speculated on the best and fastest route to get to Texas.

A man at the other pump overheard the two girls talking; he was all scruffy to say the least. His salt-and-pepper hair was so messy. His beard looked like it had never been trimmed. He leaned on the back of his beat-up old truck and smiled at the two of them. He had a passenger who looked pretty rough, possibly the hungover look, although he was drinking a beer in the truck while waiting. Then the man pumping the gas spoke.

"I couldn't help overhearing you girls talking about the best route from here to get to Texas. Most people stay on route 40, because that is the only way they know of. But we're from the area, and let me tell you of a much better and shorter way. It will save you at least an hour if not more."

"Yeah, I don't know," Fiona replied with caution. But Rachael was excited. "Oh, come on, Fiona, they're nice enough to offer." So they both got into the car and proceeded to follow the two men in the old beat-up pickup truck. Fiona still had doubts, and just a feeling of "you better be careful." She didn't know why she felt that way, but her gut kept giving her an uneasy feeling, like women's intuition.

Tori was sending her these gut feelings, trying to warn Fiona of the danger she was about to encounter. Because of this, she memorized every turn while following those men, so she wouldn't get lost.

It started to feel like they were being led into a maze as the road turned to dirt roads in the deep dark woods. Fiona was leery and kept some distance. The truck they were following pulled over, and the driver began to wave his arm out of the window for the girls to go ahead of them.

Suddenly, Fiona's heart fell into her throat and stomach, giving her an awful feeling, and she didn't hesitate to react and get the hell out of there and fast! Her inner being thought they could get killed out there, and everyone would say, "What were they doing in the middle of the forest?" Before Rachael realized what was happening, Fiona spun the car around so fast like a professional, hauling ass, stepping on the gas pedal, leaving an enormous dust cloud on the dirt road, blinding the men in the truck. She never let up, speedily remembering every left or right turn, eventually getting back onto the main road again leading to the highway. Fiona felt lucky and her life flashed before her eyes.

"Wow! Somebody must be watching over us! Rachael, do you realize that we could've been murdered out there and never found!"

"No shit, huh?" Rachael answered. "Everyone would've been wondering why we were out there in the first place! In the middle of the woods!" She scratched her head, wondering what the hell just happened! They were shook up for a long while and realized what a close call they had, and it taught them both a valuable lesson, to be careful, and don't trust just anybody. (You're not in Kansas anymore, Dorothy!)

"We are staying on route 40 the whole way from now on," Fiona stated plainly.

So they drove on, reaching the Texas Panhandle. Once again, Tori had to intervene to keep her sister safe from evil's dangers. But for now, Fiona was safe, and Tori was relieved too and could rest as her purpose was fulfilled, to keep Fiona from harm. Fiona always seemed to find trouble, even when she wasn't looking for it. So Tori's guidance was a true blessing. Heaven-sent.

After the incident, they finally let it go, calmed down, making progress on that long, boring drive. They had promised one another that they would not separate no matter what.

They made it to Amarillo, Texas, in the middle of nowhere! They were exhausted after driving sixteen hours straight—especially Fiona, after doing all the driving. She was seeing cross-eyed. Fiona could see a hotel in the far distance as she unconsciously stepped on the gas in anticipation. Not realizing how fast she was going, she passed a parked police car, speeding, and then the siren came on behind her. So she pulled over, and took her speeding ticket gracefully like a man, knowing she was in the wrong.

The girls stopped at that hotel they could see in the distance, and paid for one room. They were lucky, because the hotel only had one room left, and it only had a queen-size bed. But they didn't care and took it in a heartbeat. They showered and relaxed, and then went to the restaurant they saw from the lobby.

They were so relieved to be off the roads, and were tired and hungry. They both ordered hot open-faced turkey sandwiches and beer. But they were surprised to be denied any beer, since it was a dry county.

"Oh no, you're kidding!" Fiona exclaimed, needing a cold one after the day she had. "We've been driving sixteen hours today and got a speeding ticket and everything, and we really could have used a cold beer."

And then the waitress said, "You have to be a member to go in the hidden bar room for an alcoholic beverage and to eat food in there." So Fiona asked her how to become a member, and the waitress stated, "Well, you have to be staying at this hotel. You have to pay a dollar to become a member."

"So sign us up!" Fiona told her with relief. And they paid each their buck and entered the private, secret bar and knocked back a few cold ones till they had their fill.

The next morning the girls were refreshed, renewed after a good night's sleep. They laid the United States atlas book on the bed to plan the day's travels. This was years and years before any GPS contraptions or cell phones. It was almost the '90s now.

Out of the blue, Fiona said, "I should probably tell my parents how far we are so far. I'm sure my mother is pacing the floors right about now." Rachael agreed, always going with the flow, and they took turns using the hotel phone, each calling their parents' collect. Neither of them mentioned to their parents about the guys in the truck trying to get them lost in the woods so they couldn't escape, and who knows what else? Martha was calm on the phone, speaking in a tone of relief to hear from Fiona. Tony was proud of his daughter, showing signs of real independence and responsibility. He wasn't a worrier.

Martha worried enough for the entire family. The girls pressed on that morning, getting an early start to make some progress. Over time, they made it to Albuquerque, New Mexico. The ride through the desert was breathtaking; everything was so colorful and magical. Rachael took tons of pictures with her camera. They drove on through to Arizona. Hours had gone by when they came upon a big sign that read, *Vegas Next Exit.*

When Rachael and Fiona read it out loud, they immediately looked at each other as they burst out with laughter, yelling, "Heehaw! Right on! Here we come!" They talked each other right into a little detour to Vegas. Arizona would have to wait.

"Let's show Vegas a good time, shall we?" Fiona yelled, excited as hell for another adventure of a lifetime. They ended up in a cheap motel, Algier's. They paid for one week up front, and they got a really good deal. They couldn't believe how cheap it was and were very thankful—more money to spend at the casinos. They only checked in the motel to sleep anyways, so they didn't care. They went bar-hopping day and night.

They found seventy-five-cent drafts and ladies' night deals. They thought they'd died and gone to heaven. It was the best time, the fast lane! The flashing lights, the noise in the casinos, the crowds, the band, the buffets—it never ended!

They didn't tire, they were young spring chickens. They drank, they danced and laughed, they dined. All good. And then they drank and drank and drank to no end! Until it led them to drugging and being stupid.

Tori saw from heaven's bleachers that her little sister Fiona was notorious for acting upon impulse and thinking later, especially when she was lit! Tori knew Fiona wouldn't live to be old without her intervening time and time again to keep her safe from harm's way, and to keep her alive! Tori, like always, was ready for the challenge.

Rachael and Fiona were on the strip in Vegas for two days already. And they were just getting started. It was an early Wednesday morning, and they wanted to play the slot machines. But the slot machines played them. So they decided to head back to the motel, and got themselves ready for the pool.

Fiona couldn't decide which bathing suit to bring when she packed, so she brought all six of them. The girls swapped suits and tried a bunch of them on, until finally, Fiona kept the florescent orange two-piece on, and Rachael decided on the black-one piece with round metal rings all down the front of it, revealing her so-called cleavage, stomach, and bellybutton. It went good with her height of five feet seven inches, and her jet-black hair and bright blue eyes. They both had a decent tan just from walking the strip for two days. They had grown up together on the same street and had become like sisters over the years. Both so curious and eager. The two headed on out to the terrace overlooking the crystal blue pool from nine floors up.

"Oh my god! Would you look at that!" shouted Fiona with excitement. "Grab your towel and let's go!" she shouted as she danced in place.

"They have towels down there already. I saw them when we walked by the pool from the lobby," Rachael reminded Fiona. "All right, all right, I'm coming," Rachael told Fiona as Fiona was rushing her. "I just don't want to forget the sunblock."

"Good point," Fiona said, holding the door open as she waited patiently for Rachael. They giggled all the way down the hall until they reached the elevator, and continued giggling till they reached the lobby on the first floor. As they walked outside to the pool area, Fiona noticed right away an attractive man watching them, but she didn't make anything of it, except that he was sexy, and boy, would she have fun with that!

She was merely daydreaming, of course. She was used to getting looks; it happened all the time. The girls were both very attractive. They managed to find a good spot to spend their time, with two lounge chairs and a small table alongside the crystal blue pool that had a cave in it to hang out in under the waterfalls. Once they were too hot from sunbathing half the day, they made sure to check it out. Rachael had brought a waterproof camera for the trip, so they got to see from the waterfalls looking out. They had lots of fun going down the waterslide at the far end of the pool. Suddenly, Fiona spotted the same guy from before watching her every move once again. So she approached him with Rachael by her side.

"Hi," Fiona said as she smiled at him with those pearly whites sparkling. "I was wondering if I know you—I mean, have we met before? It's just that I've noticed you looking our way a few times, and well, here we are. I'm Fiona, and this is my best friend, Rachael." And Rachael bowed her head down in acknowledgment and waved her hand at him as to say hello.

"Hi, I'm Brandon," he answered the young strangers as he reached out to shake their hands as a formal introduction. "I just couldn't help but notice how much fun you were having when I saw you both, so I was just mesmerized by the both of you and how happy you both look." Rachael looked down as she blushed, but Fiona knew that he had an eye for her.

"So you think we're the fun type, huh? Well, as a matter of fact, we are. We know how to have fun!" Fiona said.

"What are you two drinking anyways?" Brandon asked them as he smiled, looking gorgeous.

"Pena Coladas," Rachael blurted out, "We've been drinking them all day, poolside."

Brandon waved down a waiter who took his drink order for the three of them.

"You didn't have to do that," Fiona told him.

"Oh, I do not mind, the pleasure is all mine," he said with his hand over his heart, gazing at them. And the girls accepted their drinks gracefully and went back to their lounge chairs alongside the crystal blue pool and in the direct desert sun. They enjoyed their piña coladas while they were ice-cold, and relaxed while they dried off.

They didn't get back to their room until almost 5 p.m. They each took a shower and freshened up for an exciting evening ahead. Fiona looked great with her fingernails and toenails painted a bright florescent orange just like her bathing suit. This color enhanced her opportune tan. Her luscious, long dirty-blond hair had natural highlights from the sun and framed her face nicely. Her big blue eyes were full of light, and her smile melted everyone's heart. And the laugh she inherited from her father was contagious. She was easily noticed everywhere she went, always making heads turn. Tonight, she was wearing a baby blue one-piece jumpsuit. It was beautifully soft-looking. It was made of silk, and opened freely at the pant legs, and the top was made like a low-cut halter top, exposing most of her perfectly blessed breasts, which she had intentionally prayed for, for years. Her petite, five foot two little dancer frame was perfect for this outfit.

Rachael wore a black dress (black again, of course; Rachael always wore black or white, but almost always black). It had spaghetti straps and was way above the knee. Her jet-black hair was a French braid, thanks to Fiona, and her earrings and necklace sparkled, as she put on her high-heeled shoes.

"I'm ready to go dancing somewhere tonight. How about you, Fiona?" Rachael asked.

"Oh, uh-huh! Me too!" Fiona replied. "I'm so ready to get my groove on, girlfriend! Let's go hit the town and paint it red!" She laughed hysterically, causing Rachael to burst out laughing as well. And the two of them were on their way out once again, without eating anything once again. They were in party mode and ready for some alcohol.

"Let's party!" they shouted and sang simultaneously. "Let's get this party started!" They giggled afterward.

"We should chant it, party, party, party!" Rachael stated, smiling away.

"No, forget that," Fiona said. "What are you going to have to drink tonight?" she asked.

"Um, I don't know, but I do know that I need a couple of shots."

"There you go, Rachael! You can just dance it off, girlfriend!"

"Yeah, and you'll be right there with me!" Rachael answered.

"You got it. Are you sure you're ready?" Fiona asked.

"Let's go, I'm ready," Rachael stated. And they were off and running. They decided, while walking on the sidewalk along the strip, to stop at each and every place for a drink along the way, until they got to the other end. That's a lot! But they didn't quite take it to the other end. Too many shots along the way! Fiona liked her tequila, and those sweet King Arthur's. Rachael liked a good Fireball, or some Yukon Jack, or vodka.

They were both pretty hammered. And happy! Then Brandon, the guy from the hotel pool, showed up out of nowhere, and Fiona had a weird feeling that he was watching them all along, but she told herself to stop being so paranoid (like Martha), and dismissed the thought.

"Hi, girls!" he said, smiling in his own charming way. "Oh, hi, you again," Rachael said as she turned around surprised. Fiona stayed silent. They were approaching the hotel together as they crossed the street. They all went to the bar inside and ordered drinks. He nudged his way over to Fiona and asked her politely if she would dance with him. The music was loud and the timing must've been right, because Fiona got off of the barstool and stood directly in front of him and said, "I'm ready if you are." And she raised her eyebrows a couple of times and rolled her eyes in a flirtatious way as she brushed up against him to lead him by the hand to the dance floor. He felt a spark in his pants as he watched her dance for him. She had all the right moves. He was turned on by her and was trying hard to not let his hard-on show. He nonchalantly pulled his dress shirt out of his pants to cover it up and continued to dance with her, and his rock-hard muscle of love! He was in heaven and didn't want this moment to end. Fiona was dancing freely and loosely like the true flower child she was, without a care in the world, and Brandon loved it. She walked away from the dance floor, then the music ended. She began looking for her drink and a cigarette, not realizing that she just walked away from him, and managed to strike up a conversation.

"You girls really do like to drink, huh?"

"We like to do a lot of things," Fiona answered."

"We'll try anything once!" Rachael added.

"Would you two be interested in smoking some pot?" He had to ask.

"Are you kidding?!" Fiona asked. "We're always interested in smoking a joint!" she concluded, continuing to ask him, "Can you get me a quantity, so I can have my own?"

"What's quantity?" he asked.

"Just a bag, a half ounce maybe, depending on the price and how good it is," Fiona answered. "I can spare thirty to forty dollars tops."

"All right," Brandon said, "but it's a ride from here to go get it. Do you want to take a ride with me?" he asked.

Fiona thought that maybe it wasn't a bad idea; she wouldn't want to get robbed.

"Yeah, I guess so," Fiona told him. "But I have to ask Rachael." She turned to Rachael smiling, and right away Rachael told her she wanted to try the slot machines. But Fiona really wanted to score a bag, so she told Rachael, "Good luck and have fun, and we'll meet up right here in an hour." Rachael agreed, waving goodbye already. So the girls parted their ways for the first time ever! Drunk! In Las Vegas! Tori knew this was a bad idea, but the girls were too intoxicated to know better. Fiona and Brandon weren't gone for two seconds before some ruffian sat next to Rachael to play the slot machine. Meanwhile, Fiona followed Brandon down a tight alley behind the casinos, with the stinky dumpsters overflowing with garbage, making the lid unable to be closed all the way.

"Yuck!" she yelled, pinching her nose closed to block the rotten smell. "Where the hell are you taking me?" Brandon began to giggle.

"My car is parked on this side street up here. I just thought this would be the fastest way for you with your high heels on and everything, and having only one hour," he explained.

"Ah, thanks," Fiona said as they approached his truck. It was an old Ford, mini size, with bucket seats, and the stick shift on the floor between the seats. Fiona stumbled getting in it, but she was comfortable, far away in her own little world. She was on a mission. They drove on some grand highway with many lanes for what seemed like an hour before Fiona spoke up. "Are we there yet?" she asked, whining purposely to sound like a little kid while sighing to express that she was getting impatient now.

"Yeah," Brandon replied, "I told you it was going to be a ride, but it is the next exit." It wasn't far after the exit to the slum of a house they ultimately entered. Fiona had her badass self-act going on as she was introduced to Brandon's dealer, Ed. Ed had a full head of hair, rats' nest–looking, that covered his face. Ed was all business as he led them both into his living room. He didn't say a thing as he lit up a fat joint and passed it to Fiona. The three of them smoked it down to nothing when Ed asked her a question. "Are you high?"

"Fuck yeah!" she told him as the transaction went down. Then she turned to Brandon and said, "We should probably get going, I almost forgot about Rachael!"

"Okay, thanks, Ed, but we got to bounce, man," Brandon told him as they shook hands and Ed winked and nodded his head up and down, patting Brandon on the back with the approval of his latest catch. The ride home was long enough for Fiona to start sobering up a little.

She began to realize that she trusted a stranger and took off with him! Without Rachael! *Who knows where he could take me?* she thought. *Where on earth am I going?* As she looked toward him just a little bit, trying to do it unnoticed, she caught a glimpse in the comer of her eye of a huge hunting knife, tucked under his seat. All of a sudden, she got the scariest feeling, like on the dirt road—that he would knife her and kill her and drop her dead body off in the desert, and nobody would ever understand how she ended up there. Fiona freaked out on him in fear as she realized this guy had been popping up everywhere prior to getting her alone.

"I need to go back and find Rachael!" She then continued on to say, "I see your knife, mister, under your seat right where the safety belt buckles! So don't pull a fast one on me, because I have one too! Just keep driving, and bring me back to where you found me!"

By the time she was through, she was practically yelling. She was bullshitting him, and especially herself for being so stupid, and for leaving her best friend Rachael. He dropped her off at once after she freaked out on him, and she told him boldly to stay away from her and from Rachael from now on, no more running into them coincidentally, and that she was onto his tricks, and she didn't like it one bit.

It was a lucky break this time with the help of Tori's intervention, for she knew the real danger that had awaited Fiona. That man had every intention of holding her at knifepoint at some point in time to control her, and rape her, as he strangled her to her last breath. But divine intervention intervened once again through Tori, from God Almighty. You better believe Fiona was once again kept safe from danger. If she only knew what was about to happen. Deep down she did know what a close call that was, and she also knew that someone up there had to be looking out for her.

She had a walk ahead of her since she got out of the truck the minute they reached the strip. The sun had gone down many hours before, and Fiona could now walk barefoot on the cool sidewalk. She carried her sandals and didn't stop anywhere until she found Rachael. She still had that ruffian creep hanging off her, and Fiona didn't hesitate to tell him to take a flying fuck! She grabbed her best friend Rachael, apologizing wholeheartedly for leaving her alone in the casino half the night.

"Would you relax?!" Rachael told Fiona. "I'm the one that wanted to stay, remember?" She slurred badly.

"I know," she said, "but let's not do that again, okay?"

"Okay." And they left together arm in arm.

"I think that it's time that we left Vegas."

"Off to bigger and better adventures!" Rachael shouted, raising her glass, spilling her drink all over her hand. She finished the rest and set the empty glass on a table as they walked out of the casino, toward the lobby with the main elevator to the rooms.

Fiona had to hold Rachael up to walk, but she thought it was because of the alcohol. They approached the old elevator with an operator in it to shut the wire cage over the door, and he asked, "What floor?"

"Number 9, I think?" Rachael questioned herself. They reached their room exhausted. Rachael fell onto the bed and ended up passing out in her short sexy black dress, and all that gaudy jewelry she liked. But Fiona laid there half the night with her eyes wide open, thinking about how it didn't take her long at all to get herself into trouble, especially feeling bad about getting drunk, and being so stupid trusting anyone. Now that could've been a bad, ugly ending. She swore to herself that she would smarten up, and prayed. Fiona was brought up with a strong and powerful faith from the time she was little. She knew how to put her faith to work. And she was certain that she didn't get out of that mess alone. She finally rolled over and allowed herself to fall asleep. Rachael lay lifeless from the date rape drug the ruffian character slipped in her drink, just before Fiona found her. She had arrived just in time.

Fiona was the first one awake the following morning. She didn't feel hung over as bad as she thought she would, so she assumed that it had to be because she sobered up before she fell asleep. Rachael, on the other hand, was a different story. She had passed out drunk. She moaned and groaned when Fiona opened the curtains, letting all the bright sunshine come in.

"Ah! What are you doing to me?" she cried. "Oh my god! It's too bright!" Fiona backed up, walking away from the window. She turned on the television as it was broadcasting a movie called *Romancing the Stone,* which she loved to watch over and over again back home, because it had a part in it where they showed a crashed plane from years before, which they found in the jungle, and when they went into the plane, they found an old album, or maybe it was a magazine, of the Grateful Dead. Fiona liked that part of the movie, being a deadhead herself. She was a hippy and proud of it.

"Let's go Rachael!" Fiona said as she raised her voice in a stern tone so that Rachael would know she was serious and meant now.

"What's the hurry?" Rachael asked. "We got no place to go."

"Well, after last night, I want out of here. Let's blow this popsicle stand!" Fiona said, trying to make light of the situation. She had already decided that they were leaving. "I'm all packed, and I suggest you do the same before I leave your ass here!"

"All right, all right! I'm up!" Rachael walked to the bathroom while holding her head. She closed the door behind her, took a shower, and came back out with her hair still wrapped in a towel. She began drying her hair with it when Fiona told her to hurry it up.

So Rachael quickly combed it out, threw all of her belongings in her bag, and headed for the door, all discombobulated. Rachael opened the door and asked Fiona, "Are you almost ready? Because I am."

"You're so cute, Rachael," Fiona told her as she giggled. "That's why I love you so much!" And then the two of them were on their way again to who knows where.

It was still morning, and it was a nice sunny day as usual in Nevada. And you could hear in the distance the roar of a train as its whistle blew an echo across the plains and off the mountains. Once the girls were on the road again, Fiona was feeling confident about choosing to leave sin city. *What happens in Vegas stays in Vegas,* she thought, also thinking about how her drinking always got her in trouble. She was always thinking of her next move, forgetting to savor the now. And the thought of contacting her parents to let them know her whereabouts and that she was all right occupied her mind. Up until now, the thought had never crossed her mind. "Miss Independent."

She was happy anywhere really. She was like a butterfly, she could live anywhere. It was amazing that Fiona found the main road for which needed to leave this area. They passed many restaurants, small businesses, and big ones too, and a gas station at every corner. It suddenly clicked in Fiona's mind that she should probably pull into one of these gas stations and fill up the gas tank. You don't want to run out of gas in the middle of the desert! She was driving a used Chevy Citation which was good on gas, and it ran great. They pulled into the very next gas station, which just so happened to be at the top of a very large hill that had fabulous views of Lake Mead in the distance, and all the mountains surrounding it glowed from the sunrise shining a reflection off of them. It was breathtaking! It didn't faze Rachael, but Fiona was of one with nature; she appreciated things like that, and always tried to savor these moments.

"Rachael, wait!" Fiona shouted over the howling wind. "Here's a twenty, can you tell the guy to turn the pump on?" It was only a matter of minutes when the gas started to flow. As Fiona pumped the gas, she noticed an odd fellow staring at her, and all she could think was *Here we go again!* He was standing next to his car, just standing there watching her every move. Fiona looked away and thought she should stop being so paranoid (like Martha) all the time, and figured her mother must be rubbing off on her. Oh no, what a thought! She never realized that her gut feelings were accurate every time because of the divine intervention from the Holy Spirit and from Tori, which she was blessed with. And thank God for that, because her instincts were usually pretty accurate. Her gut told her that this man was a creep. But don't judge. Everyone is different. *I have just issues,* she thought.

The pump stopped at twenty dollars, and Fiona put the nozzle back into its place, put the gas cap back on, and got back into the car. Rachael was still in the store, but nobody pulled up to the gas pump behind Fiona, so she didn't bother to move the car. She waited for Rachael while listening to the radio, until she came out of the store with a big brown paper grocery bag of goodies. Fiona giggled and started the car from where that creepy guy watched her every move, just staring. He looked like Prince. He began to slowly get into his car, which was a newer black Chevy Chevelle, with fat beefy tires and tinted windows. The car reminded Fiona of the movie *Christine*. Fiona had her eye on his every move, and was well aware of him as she drove away, and Rachael had no clue whatsoever. The man in the car let her go first, giving her a head start as he followed in the distance, but Fiona saw what he was doing in the rear-view mirror. She was on to him.

"I got the munchies bad!" Rachael shouted.

"Yeah, I see that!" Fiona replied laughing. "What do you got in there?"

"It's a bag of tricks!" Rachael chuckled. "They're magically delicious," she sung.

"Let's see, we got Reese's Pieces, or M&M's. We got Slim Jims and Tootsie Rolls, and some potato chips and Devil Dogs."

"Holy shit, Rachael! Good job! I'll have some chips. Did you get us anything to drink?"

"Of course," Rachael replied, "take your pick, we got Starbucks iced coffee or Mountain Dew."

"Well, which one do you want, Rachael?"

"It don't matter to me," she replied. "Then okay, I'll have the iced coffee."

"You got it. Here, I'll even open it for you, Fee." Fiona noticed that they were still being followed, so she told Rachael.

"But don't worry, I'll lose him," she told her. Rachael got scared, and Fiona's adrenaline was getting up there when it began to become a speed chase.

"This isn't funny, Fiona!" Rachael said loudly as her nervousness made her voice crack.

"Okay, I know!" Fiona answered her. She noticed the area was becoming more settled up ahead, so she stepped on the gas pedal and gained more distance from this creep. So Fiona shut the headlights off and swerved the car quickly to the right, between some tall bushes off the road, and hid there, shutting the car off. They hid and waited there and held their breath as they watched him speedily pass by. They both breathed a sigh of relief, but they were truly scared.

"This isn't funny," Rachael said.

"No shit, Sherlock!" Fiona answered as they grabbed each other and looked into each other's eyes in sheer fear. Fiona started the car and backed the car out of the bushes and back onto the main road and decided to point the car back into the direction from which they came. "Let's go this way so we don't run into him again," Fiona said. "I'm sure we can go another way."

"It's okay with me, Fee," Rachael agreed. "That was scary! Holy shit!" They were pretty shaken up, and Fiona thought that was nothing more than another miracle.

*Somebody is definitely watching over me.* It was getting to be noontime by now when they came upon the Hoover Dam. They took some pictures from the car but didn't stop. They drove on. Then they finally approached some signs that read *Grand Canyon Sixty Miles.* They were excited to go there, and there was no need for discussion if they were going or not. It was a given.

"You know, Rachael, we left Vegas a night early and are at least now in Arizona, so if you want to, let's stop at the campground here coming up. It looks like fun, look at the sign. Oh, how cute, it says, 'Welcome to the Flintstones Campground.'"

"I don't care. We can if you want to," Rachael replied agreeably. "Look, they have lean-tos, all we need is our sleeping bags."

"Yeah, if we need them at all. It was a hot day today, it's one hundred and four degrees right now."

"Yeah, no shit!" Rachael giggled. They got to a campsite and just relaxed and decompressed for a little while as they tried to look at the old map again spread out on the picnic table for their next destination. They wanted to see the Grand Canyon. It was less than an hour away.

"You know what we should do?" Fiona asked. "We should leave here tomorrow morning about eight o'clock, and get to the Grand Canyon by nine thirty, let's just say. We could check it out for a few hours," she reasoned, "and take lots of pictures no doubt, and then we only have to drive a couple of hours to Sedona."

"Sounds like a good enough idea to me, Fee. Whatever you want, you know I'm in," Rachael stated, "but I thought you wanted to spend the whole day at that Slide Rock place in Sedona that you had circled on the map?" Rachael asked, not caring either way.

"Yeah, that is true. All right, so we'll stay somewhere at the Grand Canyon tomorrow night, then we won't have to rush at all. And we'll just leave early in the morning, so we can arrive in Sedona still early in the day."

"Okeydokey," Rachael said.

"Good," Fiona said, "then it's settled." So Fiona folded up the map and put it back in the glove box of her Chevy Citation so she wouldn't lose it. She reached for her backpack on the floor in the back seat and pulled it out of the car. She unzipped the inside pocket and pulled out the bag of weed she had scored in Vegas. It made her think of the stupid dangerous chance she took, putting them both in danger like that. She sat at the picnic table and rolled a fat joint that she intended on smoking right away.

"Want to go for a walk?" she asked Rachael. As she looked at Rachael, she held the perfectly rolled joint up to her face.

"No thanks," Rachael answered, "none for me, I'm still hanging, I'm never doing shots again!"

Fiona laughed. "Where have I heard *that* before?"

"Besides, Fee, there's people everywhere! And kids! And that stuff reeks, man!"

Fiona nodded her head and just got into the car and began rolling up the windows. She started the engine and put the air-conditioner on high, then before long, she was high. When she was through, she got out of the car, and a huge cloud of smoke accompanied her. Rachael laughed, and then asked Fiona a question.

"Now what? Now what, Fee?" But as she was asking, Fiona was walking passed her with her florescent orange bikini bathing suit already in hand.

"Oh, never mind," said Rachael. "I think I already know. Hold up!" she shouted, and Fiona waited while Rachael searched her bag for her bathing suit.

"There's bathrooms right over there where we can change, and I saw a huge pool on the way in," Fiona stated.

"Woohoo!" Rachael yelled. "I got it! Ready! Set! Go!" And she hustled to catch up to Fiona. Rachael changed into her bathing suit and the two of them spent a couple of hours swimming and sunbathing before they decided to grab something to eat at the little store within the campground. They both ordered Italian grinders (subs), and ring dings, and a bundle of wood for the fire pit, and didn't forget the beer.

"Wait!" Fiona shouted. "We got to go back in for the drinks. We're going to want to drink tomorrow at Slide Rock. We can get some ice and they'll be fucking awesome and ice-cold." They put their grinders in the car and went back into the store for some more alcohol. Fiona bought a twelve-pack of Beck's and she bought a couple of nips of Bailey's and vodka for her morning coffee. And Rachael bought a kind of Smirnoff with raspberry flavoring that came in twelve-pack bottles. And she couldn't pass up a couple of nips of her favorite Yukon Jack, what else? Just in case. They managed to fit all of it in the cooler.

They drove until they found a great pull-off area next to a babbling brook or a small river where they could eat their subs. They ended up spending almost two hours there, taking it all in. They eventually made their way back to the famous Flintstone campground, two young girls without a care in the world, or even a thought of everyone back home wondering what happened to them and where could they be. All Martha could do was pace back and forth in her sullen state. All sorts of awful thoughts entered, reminding her as she put her trust in the Lord to keep Fiona safe as she stared into an abyss.

As the night turned the page of life, Martha rocked in her rocking chair as she prayed denying herself any sleep or rest. And Fiona was there in her own independent world, enjoying the bonfire she built, and started pigging out on the snacks to munch on and passing out afterwards from smoking too much pot and drinking too much alcohol, never thinking about the folks back home. They were free spirits. The next morning came without warning and poor Martha was exhausted with worry while the two spring chickens were approaching their next adventure. Martha never heard Tony as he pleaded with her to believe Fiona would be fine.

"Come on, honey! She's done this so many times and every time she's fine," he pleaded with her to listen to him, but she just sat there rocking as she held her Bible, dependent on Psalms for comfort, with that incredulous look on her face. The girls woke up fairly early, around 7 a.m. They were anxious to start a new day and drink it up all afternoon. They grabbed their small bags with their personals in them like a toothbrush, makeup, etc. But when they entered the campground bathroom, they felt uncomfortable as some women just stared watching their every move. They would just gloat and stare.

Fiona decided not to let it bother her as she went about her business. Rachael followed suit. Fiona held the screen door open with her foot as she waited for Rachael to collect all of her things. When she joined Fiona, they both walked out and Fiona let the screen door slam loudly for the bent, out-of-shape, desperate housewives.

"We weren't loud last night, were we?" Fiona asked Rachael. And Rachael had a feeling that they smelled Fiona's pot last night, so she came right out and said it.

"They probably smelled your pot."

"Maybe," Fiona replied. "Fuck them! Let's go, I want to hit the road early. We can stop for coffees along the way."

"Okeydokey!" Rachael agreed. And the girls were hitting the pavement once again. They drove until they saw signs for Sedona. The sky was so blue and the views were astonishing—majestic mountains with lines of time and history as colorful as a blessed sunset, purple and pink hues upon subtle red clay. Ancient Indian tribes that lived and died here told their life stories in hieroglyphic writings and drawings on these mountains and the presence of their spirits were felt by all. Churches to praise God were built right into the mountainsides. It was a land preserved from the spoils of man. It was clear that this land and everyone in it gave reverence and fear to the Lord our God and Creator.

The road narrowed then ended at the foot of a sacred mountain. The girls giggled about how it would crumble if they dared enter, but they had no intentions of visiting a sacred mountain. They were on a mission to find one of the best party spots there in Sedona: Slide Rock. The roads were curvy and windy as they climbed the hills and mountains.

The old Chevy kept shifting gears, making clicki-ty-clackity noises, while being careful not to crash in fear of missing the spectacular views. There were waterfalls coming down the side of this very steep mountain that back-dropped the waterfall and river town of Slide Rock. They found it! They rustled up enough money between them to pay the parking attendant. They were told that arriving early meant avoiding the traffic jam. They grabbed their beach towels and suntan lotion, and the cooler which took the both of them to carry. It was heavy and it was a little bit of a walk to reach the river, so they had to take many quick breaks putting the cooler down. Once they saw the river, their jaws dropped open. They'd never seen anything like it! The river rushed through constantly, smoothening red rocks beneath the water until the rocks became smooth enough to slide down. Sitting on it felt as though it really were a slide! But they found out that the water was as cold as ice. But the baking Arizona sun gave then good reason to get wet and splash each other and welcome the coldness. They shivered at first, but then it didn't faze them anymore.

They ran to their towels, acknowledging the fact that they were lying on hard red rock and not beach sand like they were accustomed to. And they couldn't help but notice how blue, blue could be when they looked up at the clear, cloudless skies. It was an amazing day for the two of them. It made them feel rejuvenated! And alive! They left Sedona sunburnt. It didn't seem to bother either one of them. They were headed to Phoenix until they encountered a terrible sandstorm. Neither girl had ever seen anything like it before. In fact, they couldn't see anything at all. Fiona made the mistake of putting her windshield wipers on with the rinse. What a mess it made of the windshield. It smeared the window so bad that she had no choice but to pull over with Rachael's assistance. She hung her head out the window just enough to see where they could pull over. They were in the desert mountains, and the last thing they wanted was to drive off a cliff! But danger was rooted all around them. But the living God has ordered myriads of angels to assist Tori's spirit in protecting Fiona (if Fiona only knew). The sandstorm lasted about another twenty minutes. Once the windshield was cleaned, they were off and running like the other times before and those to come.

"Rachael?" Fiona asked.

"Yeah, what?" she asked.

"I want to camp out again tonight. I just saw a sign for camping and it read the *Mogillon Rim,* something like that, and it sounds interesting."

"Fiona, you know that I don't give a shit what we do? You're driving, honey."

"I know, I know," she replied as she drove on until they finally approached the ramp. At the end of the ramp was a tunnel that went under and through the red rock mountain. It led them into tall pine trees all lined up along the road until they entered a thickly wooded area. Neither girl ever thought that they'd find pine country like this in Arizona, but its amazing contrasts were indescribable. They saw some jack rabbits chasing each other, and a cluster of deer which never blinked an eye as they watched them drive by. The road was littered with bicyclists and tourists on both sides of the road, but they were amused. "Boy, oh boy, it's kind of late in the day. I hope they're not full at the campground," Fiona stated.

"I know, huh?" Rachael answered. "Well, if it is full, we will just have to go back to that main road we were on and keep going. If we have to, we can go all the way straight through to Phoenix, Fiona. It'll just take a few hours or so. And there's plenty of hotels there."

"True," Fiona replied. They continued down the narrow, windy back road. The tall trees began to canopy the road when they came upon the entrance with a big sign that read Welcome to the Mogillion Rim Campground. Fiona parked the car in front of the trailer home with the blinking red sign that read Office Open. She went in alone to rent a campsite, while Rachael smoked her cigarette with both feet hanging out of the open window. She turned the car key back and then played the radio off of the battery. It was playing the song "Slow Ride." The driver's door opened abruptly, startling Rachael. She sat up, pulling her feet back into the car, and Fiona lowered the volume on the radio.

"How'd it go?" she asked as she blew her smoke out of the window.

"Good," said Fiona, "we got number 11. It should be the first right and then we drive around in a big circle…oh yeah, it's right there." They set up camp and took an inventory of the beverages in the cooler, and made a quick trip to the variety store that sat beside the office. They were planning to throw a few cold ones back while they sat around the campfire after dark, and before dark for that matter. Oh, how they were a sight for sore eyes. Drinking every day and every night; it was a lifestyle for them. As they relaxed around the fire, they noticed a girl in the next campsite to the right, number 13. She appeared to be all alone. And then again, she didn't. The girl noticed Fiona and Rachael were watching her, so she waved to them. Rachael and Fiona waved back and without any hesitation went over out of curiosity to introduce themselves.

"Hi, I'm Fiona, and this is Rachael."

"Hi," the girl replied, "my name is Irene. Don't mind me. I'm just feeding my furry little friend over here, see him?" she asked as she pointed over to the brush among the pine needles. She was wearing some type of knitted oversized hat that had her hair tucked away inside in the back. It was all sorts of colors. Then she had on a tank top and shorts, and hiking sandal shoes. She was maybe five feet at that, but not sure if she was even that. Her wavy blond hair framed her face, and those big blue eyes, and boy, what a smile, one that a person could never forget! And her laugh was comical. She sounded like one of the munchkins from *The Wizard of Oz*, jumping out of the flowers when Dorothy's house fell on the wicked witch of the west.

"Irene, what is it?" Rachael asked. Irene giggled like the munchkin she was. It struck the girls funny and the three of them laughed. Then Irene continued.

"I buy the big bag of raw peanuts in the shell, and I give him one at a time. He's a chipmunk, and I named him King. He even eats out of my hand, off of my shoulder, wherever I put the peanut."

"Wow, that's awesome!" Rachael raved about it.

"Yeah, but do you know what else is cool?" Irene asked them. "I come back here every year, and I take the same campsite every year, number 13, and we do this right here every year. His hole is right there by the big rock." She pointed while she spat out some peanut shells. She couldn't stop herself. She loved peanuts.

"Very cool, Irene. Very cool indeed," Fiona said, then she asked her. "Are you from Arizona? You said you come here every year."

"Yeah, I live in Phoenix," Irene answered her.

"Huh? We're going there tomorrow." And the three of them talked for hours. Rachael and Fiona laughed at all of Irene's deadhead stories, just the way she told them was funny, with that laugh on top of it! That's what she called herself, a deadhead. That was what they called the followers of the band the Grateful Dead. Some of those deadheads were in deep, and looked up to Gerry Garcia like he was a god. Irene managed to sell them some jewelry she had made herself, in quantities to sell at the shows (the concerts) to help support the costs to follow them from state to state, following the band when they toured. And they exchanged names and addresses and phone numbers, to keep in touch. No such thing as cell phones yet. The girls were both more than appreciative for the marijuana sample she gave them to try out, which she grew herself.

They all hated to call it a night, but the time was late, and Rachael kept yawning while tears ran down her face, consistently wiping them away. She was stoned out of her tree and was ready to crash. And Fiona was toast. They walked back to their campsite and turned in. The only thing they could hear was the crackling of the fire as it died down. The ambers in the fire pit glowed as brightly as the stars above, and the shadow danced in the night as darkness wrapped its arms around the forest. Blue spruces were towering over their campsite. Then they heard footsteps walking toward them, making Fiona sit up to take a peek. It was Irene.

"Hi, hope I didn't scare you," Irene said.

"What's up?" Fiona asked her. Irene giggled with that awesome smile.

"I wanted to tell you guys to go and see the herd of elk at the bottom of the ravine. There's a fence that starts behind the last campsite. If you follow it, it'll take you to the dam that controls this lake. Right now, everything is dry and they feed there. Try to catch them in the dam, before you two take off. That's it! Drive safe! Bye!" And Irene turned around and walked back to her campsite.

Fiona crawled back into her sleeping bag and had no trouble falling asleep. Rachael didn't have a problem falling asleep either. They both felt refreshed when they awoke in the morning. They just needed some rest. They took Irene's advice and took a sneak peek of the elk. Rachael had her camera, and they did see some elk. They watched them graze the dry riverbed with all kinds of things for the elk to choose from. But once the girls were noticed by the elk, they began slowly walking toward the girls, which in turn, made the girls back off and back up until they were once again at the top of the hill feeling safe. Rachael got some pictures, never letting go of Fiona the whole time. Rachael was far from brave and had never experienced the presence of a wild animal. Fiona could switch her bravery on and off; girly girl one minute or a tomboy the next. It was, though, a memory they wouldn't soon forget. In fact, Fiona enjoyed the wilderness so much that she stalled to leave until finally Rachael lost her patience with her.

"Fine!" Fiona yelled. "But I don't know what the big hurry is. Checkout time isn't till eight forty-five."

"Fiona, you're the one who said you wanted to hit the fucking road early!"

"Yeah, yeah," she fussed as she answered Rachael and they walked to the car. "Do you have everything, Rache?" Fiona asked.

"Well, there isn't a fucking thing left on the campsite, so yeah!" she answered irritably as she got into the car.

"All right, Rachael, don't be mad at me anymore," Fiona begged.

"Well, I hate it when you make me hound you to go! You told me to!" Rachael said calmly as she raised her voice slightly, trying to get her point across.

"You're right, I'm sorry," Fiona replied, "and thank you. That's why I love you so much." She went on with soft, gentle love tap-punches to Rachael's arm. "Here, have a butt." And Rachael gladly accepted, and things were back to usual. Little did either of them know, but it was actually Tori and her legion of angels who were stopping

Fiona from going anywhere too soon, for danger awaited up ahead. But there wasn't any way for Fiona or Rachael to know that.

Being held back kept them both from what could've been multiple fatalities on the freeway. As they drove upon the Verde Valley, the scenery overwhelmed them to no end! The desert mountains were endless and timeless. Saguaro cacti, which grew at least twenty feet tall, were scattered everywhere, and they were all in bloom with rings, and atop of them were big white funnel-shaped flowers. So many colors blanketed the desert. The dangerous roads swerved atop the mountain. They saw their first roadrunner! Fiona stopped at the next rest area to take some pictures. They were at a very high elevation and the wind blew around, whipping a hot breeze against their skin. They kept grabbing their hair as it blew in their faces and sometimes in their mouths.

"Ha-ha, woohoo!" Fiona screamed above the howling wind as she grabbed for her hat on her head. Rachael wore a bandana as a kerchief and the point on it kept flopping into her face in perfect sync with the gust of wind. Fiona was trying not to piss her pants; she was laughing so hard. They laughed happily together. "Holy shit, Rache!" Fiona yelled at the top of her lungs to be heard over the whipping wind. "I wouldn't want to be lost out there! You'd be lucky to make it out of there alive!"

"You're not shitting, huh?" she replied, holding her breath at the awful thought of it. In the meantime, a car pileup was occurring just before the very next exit! Apparently, there were pieces of a blown tire in the fast lane. Two young guys in a car swerved to miss it, except the driver cut the wheel too fast and too sharp, or all of the above, nobody really knows. But they caused a car pileup and many were lucky to be just shaken up. The two guys ended up flipping the car over, and it slid on its roof quite a distance as it ejected the both of them, like Jonah being spit out of the whale's mouth, but through the back window.

If Tori hadn't held Fiona back this morning at the campground dam, she wouldn't still be here, or anywhere. Rachael too for that matter. They were both alive and well, because of divine intervention. And yet they had no idea.

They didn't stay atop the mountain for too long, it was much too windy and noisy. And Fiona needed to smoke a joint. They both jumped back into the Chevy Citation, rolled the windows up to about three quarters of the way, and sparked up a big fatty. Thirty minutes passed before Fiona started the car, turning on the AC while rolling up the windows, and put it in drive, and there they were, off again to new adventures. No fear. No clue.

They were not held up by the traffic due to the accidents. One lane remained open so cars could keep moving. The way had been opened for them.

The spectacular views were a great distraction to the lengthy ride. They took their time, stopping here and there for a bite to eat or a bathroom break, or to take a picture in the rest areas provided with a view lookout. They had no set schedule, which made it nice. It was late afternoon when the girls arrived in Phoenix.

They continued on to Tempe where Fiona knew Arizona State University was located.

They knew there'd be plenty of bars in a college town. Unfortunately, they rented a room at one of the worst hotels around, with a nasty reputation for prostitutes and pimps just like Van Buren in Phoenix. Great! (If Martha only knew! She'd be sick, never mind crying every day in fear of "What if this happened or what if that happened?" Martha would what-if herself to death if God let her. Good thing that deep within, her faith was unshakable.)

Rachael and Fiona were in their nasty hotel room, nothing fazed them; they were too young to care. It was a puny room, and vile, and gross, with old blood stains on the wall from killing flies. It even came with a complimentary flyswatter. They weren't relaxed there at all, but they needed a place for the night; everywhere else they looked in their price range was booked.

They didn't really sleep that night, keeping one eye open, and they slept on top of the bedspread, because they were disgusted and were afraid to look under the covers or through the sheets. They were courageous to stay, not really having much choice, but they got the hell out of there at the break of day to find a good place early for maybe two nights, they hoped.

Curiosity got the best of them as they both voted to drive farther to finally end up at some place called the Palms. Just so happened, they were only a few miles away from the Superstition Mountain, across from a real gold mine welcoming visitors. And Canyon Lake and Tortilla Flats were up ahead. When they heard those names, that was it, they had to check them out.

The hotel wasn't anything to write home about; it wasn't anything fancy, but compared to the last one, it sparkled! They dumped off all of their bags and belongings there before driving out to see those Superstition Mountains. They weren't prepared to hike any of the trails since they left the hotel with nothing but their three-dollar sandals and a camera. So they continued driving on, following signs to view Canyon Lake. Many pictures were taken along the way; Rachael was becoming a professional at it. There were cacti in bloom everywhere! Fiona focused on the roads, because they were very curvy like nothing she had ever seen before! If you went off this road, you could be tumbling down the steep mountainside for quite a while. Deadly, no room for mistakes. Fiona was a good driver. Her father taught her with a standard, and he used to teach her at the cemetery, because the corners were sharp for sharp turns.

"Never go on the grass!" he would say. "All tires on the road." And then he would say "Can't kill anybody here, they're already dead!" as he would grin and tease her. This memory Fiona was experiencing made her realize that she better call home pretty soon!

They drove on until they approached the lake, which couldn't be missed. It was smack in the middle of a valley of mountaintops surrounding it, blanketed with cacti and flowers of all kinds and colors, and birds everywhere! Their view was from above the lake.

The road descended into a beach area. They lay out there and swam. It was magnificent. It was next to a campground, but they already had a room at the Palms near

Apache Junction. If they had only known, but they didn't. They dried off in the sun before putting clothes on over their bathing suits. They wanted to keep going to see the Trading Post in Tortilla Flats, population seven. It was only a little farther down the road which descended deeper into the valley. So they did their touristy thing, and then went back to the hotel room. After they showered, they were ready for something more.

There was a community fire pit for all the guests at the hotel to hang out at night. And they joined strangers and they all got drunk together. Neither girl had very good judgment when they were drinking—and hardly ever when they were sober for that matter! Were they really ever sober? The next thing you know, they are in different hotel rooms, with different strangers, all wanting to sell them this drug or that to try. There's the youth making all the wrong choices, you know, the ones with all the answers.

And all the while, nobody back home, not even their friends, have heard from either of them, and they are fearing the worst, stressed out to the max.

And there is Martha, resenting Fiona's lifestyle, turned inside out with fears of the worst, or even if Fiona's heart became besmirched, ever letting her guard down again. She took advantage of every opportunity to still the body and quiet the mind, allowing herself to slip between the cracks of the outer world into the inner one of silence, coming away from prayer renewed in body and mind and soul, and at peace with herself. Martha clung to her Bible as she read Psalms for comfort—not one word to her or Tony.

Tony just paced the floor, holding steady, knowing his little girl would pull something off to fix all this. In the past, their surprise knew no bounds as deep silence enveloped them. Truth is that nobody anywhere has heard anything from either one of them, or seen them anywhere. Now the whole neighborhood, family, and friends were fearing the worst.

The girls always forgot about everybody else while they were continuing to party with strangers. And suddenly, they were paying for nights at the same hotel so they could stay longer, so that they could make many more drug connections with even more strangers! They had no clue that they were slowly slipping away from reality and losing their way, drifting from the light. Their life was about to become a slow death! Once they glowed with spirit and light and hope! Now they were as dull as a pencil or wilted, dead flowers. They chose a path without a lamp to light their way. How dreadful! All the while, Tony was back home counseling and consoling Martha, day after day.

"You know how Fiona is! We always worry for nothing in the end! She never ceases to amaze us!" he'd plead with her. Martha's faith was what held her upright through it all. And then there was Tori, who was on standby as she waited for her backup of angels and the Word to be spoken. Then and only then could they step in to help Fiona. It had been weeks since the girls left home.

When they ran out of money, it was a very sobering experience. They couldn't even get home now! "Good going, Buck Owen!" as Tony would say. But they still had wheels, thanks to dear old dad. So they slept in the car at night. Their circle of friends changed like the days in a calendar, left out in the wind. It was a life of self-destruction. A learned behavior? Or a pattern? A habit? Addiction? What? Who knows? Life rubs away at different people in different ways with different outcomes, like the potter shaping the clay. The way the clay is touched determines the outcome, or its shape. That's what gives each of us our own impression, from one standpoint, because of our experiences, which hopefully, eventually shape us to come to God. That is his will. Their circle of friends kept changing as their lives began to change, due to the decisions they made, and wrong choices along the way to get to this homeless point. It also meant hanging with a different crowd and meeting different dealers. They could sell drugs to make money, so they ought to. But these two girls never saw danger in anything anywhere! They were so naive and impressionable, and now most times and under some type of influence, easily persuaded.

They made a deal with some sleazeball to sell a gram of cocaine a day for him, and that could pay their way to sleep at his place, including a shower a night. So they did that every day, to have a place to sleep every night. They could not see the dangers of this whole arrangement at all! They were so, so young, not knowing how bad the world could be out there. Wolves in sheep's clothing led the lambs to slaughter! And all Tori could do was watch and wait in faith.

# *Chapter 14*

OVER THREE WEEKS HAD PASSED before Fiona's parents ever heard a word from her. Tony was not happy with her at all, and he wasn't afraid to let her know it! Martha, on the other hand, was furious! She was afraid to say the wrong thing. She felt like she was at Fiona's mercy; she didn't even ask her to come home. She knew Fiona too. And, if she asked her to come home, why, she would just stay out there longer!

They were told that the girls both worked at the same McDonald's together, and that they had a hotel room, and they were just working to stay longer and explore the area. So the emotions rose high at the initial knowledge of both the girls being okay, and then down to the lowest of lows to the news that they weren't returning. At least not yet. This wasn't over at all. They didn't know the half of it. But Tori did.

Time marched on as they turned over a gram each a day for the sleazeball who called himself "Sly." When the girls tried some of his stuff, they liked it. So they had to sell more of it to pay for the night to sleep there, and to snort some and not have to pay for it. Things were beginning to unravel as they faded into the abyss, as time gained speed, until it spiraled out of control.

Fiona and Rachael got lost in the adventure. What started out as fun turned into the girls needing a fix! You could throw responsibilities out the window. Good luck with that! It was obvious to Tori as she watched them from the bleachers of heaven that they were completely incapable of pulling themselves out of this one. And Tori could see what it was doing to her parents. They were at their wit's end! And she didn't like it. They didn't want to call the cops, because they both knew that this was Fiona, free-spirited and her own boss, and stubborn, not seeing the harm in it. The tighter they would squeeze, the further she would run, feeling smothered. Martha couldn't help it. But if they didn't call the police and something happened, how would that feel? How would that look?

Martha began missing a lot of work, being too nervous and anxious, and suffered all those sleepless nights. Tony, well Tony was mad, downright pissed off, plain and simple. Tori couldn't wait to send help to the rescue. But, as always, she had to wait for the Word. Until then, Tori paced above the clouds, swooping back and forth amid the clouds of all dimensions. Her courage stirred within her spirit, as her bottled energy yearned to burst colors of power and might! Fiona simultaneously felt a breeze causing a chill up her spine.

Tori whispered in the wind, "I'm coming, Fiona!" She cried. "I wish you could hear me!" she stressed. Then Tori turned toward the heavens as she prayed to the Creator of all things, the living God, vowing to give back to the world, which was meant to be beautiful and pure.

"Lord!" she cried. "You ripped me from my mother's breasts. An ill infant, you called me home to you. But how can I show that love is the answer to those I have left behind, if I cannot call on you to show them that this if true? Please, Father," Tori prayed, "Fiona has never met me and I am her sister. I lived and died before she was ever born, and yet she never left my name, Tori, or my memory, out of any conversation, feeding my spirit, always sounding proud to be my sister, so that I will never be forgotten. So I owe her life, as you meant it to be. I ask you for your help, because with God all things are possible." Tori finished her prayer as she zipped around her dominion.

Everyone back home was starting to believe that maybe Fiona did run away.

Rachael's mom never called looking for her. Martha found that odd. But then again, come to think of it, she never met her. Martha and Tony's house was the neighborhood hangout, so they never got a home phone number from Rachael. Come to think of it, they really didn't know a cotton picking thing about Rachael! Martha's heart dropped into the pit of her stomach as she became overloaded with worry. She felt her heart pounding away as she began to realize just how serious this really was. Fiona was barely eighteen, and she was who knows where! Martha felt like she lost another daughter. She was crushed, feeling as though her burning heart had turned to soot and smoldering smoke. Next would be the bucket of water to end it all!

Martha began to pray for Fiona while she locked herself in her room. She couldn't stop thinking about how not one soul had seen Fiona or Rachael in a long time. *They could be anywhere,* she thought. Martha reached for a tissue as she cried, only to find the box empty. She opened the top drawer of her dresser and took a handkerchief out that was given to her by her mother, Elise, Fiona's grandmother. It had been given to Elise from her mother. Martha buried her face in it, letting her emotions go as she cried and sighed, catching her breath.

Fiona, without realizing it, had reminded Martha all her life that she was a free spirit, but Martha became angry at how this emotional roller coaster could've been avoided with one simple phone call! She felt so defeated. She knew she had to stop fearing the worst! It was killing her!

Fiona had always been a rolling stone, gathering no moss. And there was a time for scattering stones, and a time for gathering stones, Martha thought as she felt an immense strength building up inside of her. Martha walked over to her dresser and looked into the mirror, continuously repeating "All is well" until she started to believe it. She knew she had to trust God to even produce faith, to be able to receive any goodness from him. And Fiona's life was in his hands after all—all of our lives.

Martha had absolutely no doubt that the girls had gotten themselves into trouble by now. It was the not knowing that was killing her. Once Martha reassessed everything and got a hold of herself, she and Tony pulled together in this crisis rather than fell apart.

They were going through enough already. This made Tori ecstatic as her spirit filled with light and glee and endless possibilities, as she burst with excitement and unquenchable joy, zooming in flight like a rocket launching off to space at the speed of light. She transformed into a cauldron of love to be filled with God's glory, until she would spill over into Fiona's life. Tori already knew but wanted Fiona to know also that with God all things are possible. Tori's insight, along with the meek diviner's capabilities, could surely cure Fiona's troubles. It would be slender and a subtle succor. And with good reason.

The girls' appetite for drugs grew fastidiously, in a lewd, obscene, and salacious manner. And Sly loved it! He promoted the lewd lifestyle as he ravished these innocent girls like lambs being led to the slaughter, not comprehending what they were caught up in. He planned to ravish them until he was glutted and full, which would be impossible to do with his appetite for ruining young lives. But he was susceptible to falling slave to his cumulative, incredulous ways of thinking. And this time would be no different.

The girls were always kept wasted, so they didn't know how much time had actually passed. To them it felt like a month; to everyone else, it was three months that had gone by. It was as though they had blindfolds on their eyes, not able to see the future or the now.

Their lifestyles became rote and senseless. Of course, they told you it was a propitious time, as though between two rocky crags with no way out. Anything to justify the uncouth way they lived. And they had the nerve to gloat and stare at others. They acted churlish and mad at the world, a couple of stubborn louts! They were angry yet sullen, never noticing time lapsing. They'd surface now and then with recurrent phone calls. Martha and Tony appreciated it very much! They never dared tell Fiona what she should do or what she shouldn't do. That would only keep her away from home longer.

And they wanted her home terribly and would receive her with great merriment! But until then, Martha would keep the faith and pray for her, and Tony also would not lose all hope. If they only knew that their daughter was hanging out on street comers running drugs! With ruffians! And switching friends from one day to the next, spending her life with people who don't even give two shits about her!

Tony and Martha had a vague idea of what was going on. Tony always knew when things weren't right. He always suffered from a pinging pain in his stomach, as though his moral compass was guiding him to take some action. And then his furrowed cheeks became flushed, because he knew this situation with Fiona was becoming vexatious and troublesome. He was going to put an end to being shunned by his own daughter! And his joy had reached its lowest ebb. Even Fiona and her bad choices wouldn't break Tony's theism. Neither Tony nor Martha were skeptics. And they both loathed individuals who would try to make light of their most certain beliefs. To think that there are people who would actually try to abolish someone's beliefs, and then scoff at them for it! What a world! But Martha and Tony learned a long time ago to listen blithely. Let them suffer from their own blitheness, causing their own vileness as they dragged themselves through dales and valleys calling it life! What fools! To each his own. Martha and Tony always could recognize the sort, both being blessed that way and because of their undeniable faith.

Tori could hear Fiona's cries and writhes in pain and agony as she saw her pine away with guilt. And Tori could also see Fiona coming to the realization that her best friend Rachael had left her to thumb back home all alone to save herself. That's all Fiona could remember as she looked around the room full of strangers to her, lying around spread out here and there, in their own space and time.

Rachael was now a winnowed thresher to her as she remembered Rachael had left with only a few things to carry. She had nothing, and hadn't accomplished one thing—except maybe a good lesson, and the sense to return home. But Fiona was the only one who knew Rachael went back.

Tony and Martha and the boys had no knowledge of Rachael's return, until Tommy and Felicia ran into her at the River's Edge Bar and Grill. His insolence surprised Rachael, but she could understand why: because she returned without Fiona! And that made them all uneasy when Tommy told his parents the news. Martha's first reaction was to come unglued, but she had since learned how to control her initial reactions and just breathe.

Tommy also told them what else Rachael reported to him. Rachael told him excitably, as her eyes lit up.

"Tommy, I had no idea how much trouble I was in until I felt like angels came and swept me away, out of that awful place I was in." And then she also told him, "I don't know why Fiona wouldn't come with me?" But Tom didn't want to acknowledge such gibberish. The raw emotion he felt knowing his sister Fiona was out there alone somewhere, branded and sizzled his heart continuously. Rachael had also informed Tommy that Fiona and she had made it to Los Angeles, California, and that Fiona may still be there. Rachael went on about how they had gotten pulled over on the freeway for failing to use a directional while changing lanes. The police officer had made them sit in the cruiser for nearly an hour while he let the police dog sniff out the entire car. Then the cop had finally told them that the dog could smell drugs. But the only drugs they had at the time were already either smoked, snorted, or ingested.

The police officer eventually had to let them go when Fiona remembered to tell him that she bought the car used, so it could've been the previous owner. He was satisfied knowing that his canine partner could've definitely found something, if there was in fact something to find. So they lucked out that time. He stopped hassling them and finally let them go. But that happened way before California, Rachael reported. Now the big question was, does Fiona still have the car? Well, it was a good place to start. Knowing how featherbrained Fiona could be was enough reason for worry, but the task of finding her would churn up mire. Fiona's habit of flitting about with friends also would make it difficult to pin her down. Her wanton lifestyle would surely endanger her eventually, if it hadn't already.

Martha and Tony knew that they had to remain pitiless if they were ever going to be able to really help Fiona. Being stouthearted would be the best options. Fiona was just a free-spirited, young, and naive infidel. Her agnosticism was not practiced by her parents. They would handle her like a fragile flower, clinging tightly to each petal, in hopes of it not withering away. That is, if they could find her.

# *Chapter 15*

TONY WAS HELL-BENT ON TAKING a road trip with Donny and Tommy to California in search of Fiona. They discussed their options, and tried to devise a plan if they did get lucky enough to find her, especially in case if she wouldn't come home with them willingly. The last thing they wanted was a farce, a fiasco—Fiona's fiasco. With impeccable planning, they would prepare themselves for her defiant reaction. Fiona would immediately accuse all of them of being mettlesome. It pained them all to think of her as a wandering vagabond! They would converge upon her acting pious, and they would brazenly prevail! Fiona would never embrace a vexatious approach. It would be stifling. She would not be manhandled and would rebuke all attempts and smite them instantly. Without doubts, they all agreed.

The day came when Tony and the boys headed west in search of their beloved Fiona. Tommy felt positive that they'd find her, while Tony and Donny highly doubted it.

Tony didn't have a good feeling deep down in his gut, which scared him immensely, considering he wasn't a worrier. It was a dark and cloudy morning as the three of them went off. Martha waved goodbye from the driveway as her heartstrings bowed like flags in the wind, as she wiped her tears away with her mother's handkerchief. The wind began fiercely whirling over the windswept mountains to the west. Martha knew God would help to topsy-turvy Fiona's plans of isolation and despair; she prayed they'd find her mired in problems. She didn't want to fear the worst, but instead, hoped for the best.

Fiona's lifestyle had become an anathema. Dark places and shady people were liars to her. The domino effects of all her poor choices and careless decisions had left her broken and expecting the worst all the time. No wonder her channels of positive energy were blocked, unable to seep in—a definite rejection of willingly receiving it. How awful!

Fiona concocted ways, and groped for her flippant lies, to defend her new lifestyle, rushing pell-mell down like a drunkard, not even fathoming the intensity of the entire ugly situation she was in, and the big picture, spending her time getting "messed up," wasted, and even neighing for the others' stash! She didn't know how many of them whatsoever were also hiding out and squatting in some house tucked away in the center of LA., which should've been deemed inhabitable. This house Fiona was in was shambles; all the doors dividing rooms were gone. Missing. The walls were covered in graffiti with dates of when this guy or that guy was here, and phone numbers, messages written on the wall in hopes of reaching someone. People just laid themselves out, scattered about on the floor, and in comers and down the stairway in their ecstasy. Nobody ever really talked to the other guy. It was just a space off the street for anybody to come in and fly high. What an existence!

Some were criminals in hiding, and some were junkies in hiding. It was a shelter, no place for a sweetheart like Fiona. She's just gotten in over her head.

Fiona has always been like a bird seeking an islet, looking for a place to fit in, but the vileness of this existence was repulsive. Indeed she was in need of divine intervention! Fiona's fleshy being was not intended to rot in this way; it was intended to soar like an eagle! This onslaught of the oppressor certainly needed to be abated. And it was no surprise to Tori's spirit when she heard the oppressor scoff at the idea as he whispered obscenities to try to silence her efforts.

Tori's indignation left him feeling bereft and full of frustration, and for now that would be his indictment. Tori knew that her help mattered immensely in saving her sister Fiona, her sister who lifted her up on a daily basis, acknowledging her short existence to everyone she met, even though the two sisters had never met. But Tori saw Fiona as the lost soul, and not the other way around. His dilemma was by no means over.

Fiona's free will balanced the act. She had to want to go or Tori's hopes would soon dry up like a stream in the desert, and Fiona would be washed away down the rivers of hopelessness and despair. The girl who once had so much to offer, so much to give. But she could never find anyone worthy of receiving all she had to give, and all that she had to offer. Just like the old saying goes, "Right church, wrong pew." She always trusted the wrong people, unsavory characters and ruffians whom she always thought that she could help!

Tony and the boys arrived in Los Angeles after driving across the country for five days total. They took turns driving. They were uncomfortable and cranky. They were on edge and very serious about their mission to bring their baby sister Fiona home safely once and for all!

Once they found a room, they unpacked, took showers, and got some food in their stomachs, making them all much happier and clear-minded to devise some type of a game plan for the following morning's search for Fiona. They pondered upon the information given to them from Rachael. Supposedly, Fiona still had her car, so their plan was to ride around looking for her brown Chevy Citation. It would be hard to miss, since she had a sticker on the hatchback window that had florescent colors, with dancing bears that she bought at a Grateful Dead concert. But it wouldn't be that easy. Oh, they saw plenty of Citations, but to no avail! The first day of searching came up empty.

Tomorrow they would split up. Tony would walk around downtown LA, Donny would go on to the east side of town, and Tommy would search for Fiona on the west side. They had planned to meet back at the hotel at 3 p.m. And they did. But none of them saw her anywhere.

"Maybe we're not looking in the right places?" Donny questioned.

"What about the nightclubs? Maybe it's the nightlife we should be looking at?" Tommy exclaimed.

Tony replied saying, "Good point." Tony hoped he wouldn't find her stripping in some club, but then felt he'd just be happy to find her no matter what she was up to, but didn't want to imagine how bad of a mess she could really be in by now. When it came to Fiona, you never knew what was going to happen! She never ceased to amaze Tony, one way or the other. The three men talked with much anxiety half the night, trying to find right approach if they did in fact find her. Would she even recognize them? Would they recognize her? Would she talk to them? Would she leave with them? What if she told them that they needed to leave? What then? What would Martha do if they returned without Fiona? Would she turn her back mournfully? Would they seriously get through it? Seriously? Another daughter? Really? Nobody wanted that. It was a thought that kept her and the boys from giving up. They just had to find her.

They searched every nook and cranny of downtown LA separately. They decided to go forward together and not split up. And they felt safer in numbers to enter some of the worst dives they had ever seen. They were rough. And Tony and the boys weren't barhoppers to start with. Even in the bars they entered in the daytime, nobody recognized the picture of Fiona that Tony would show them, except at this one place where the bartender acted perturbed and aggravated, like he wanted to say something. Maybe he was being watched by someone and couldn't talk. That's the impression Tony got. So he and the boys left peacefully and then they went outside; they agreed that they would definitely have to return to this place.

It could be a lead. It was in a rough neighborhood and it was a tiny bar, a hole in the wall. It was called Woody's Back Door Lounge.

The sign outside was lit up in red letters, with half of them lit and blinking off and on. It had iron bars on the

windows in front by the entrance. They were a little intimi-
dated, and for good reason. They kind of feared that would
happen if they did return. But they had to, because Tony
had a gut feeling the bartender was trying to hide something or fearing something. Something wasn't right! Tony
had every intention of getting to the bottom of it.

"Dad!" Donny said, raising his voice slightly. "Those
guys could kill us! We got to go back there! Those guys
wouldn't hesitate to kill us and get rid of our bodies, and
nobody would ever know a thing! Use your head, Dad!"

"All right! All right! Take it easy! You're right! You're
right!" Tony replied as he threw his hands up in the air as
though he surrendered.

"You guys! Come on now!" Tommy interrupted. "All
we got to do is sit in the car tonight from around the
comer, and watch and hope we see Fiona." Tommy was
calm and assured them that was the answer. The best idea
so far was the conclusion, so they went back to the car
and drove until they found a restaurant, Thelma's Cafe. It
was a '50s-themed restaurant and it felt very inviting. They
really needed a bite to eat. The hired help had smiles on
their faces, and there were so many signs hanging on the
walls and pictures and model cars, and you really did get
that feel that you were back in the 1950s. They offered
huge helpings of anything you could think of. The custom-
ers inside talked among themselves raving about the place.
And they had old fashion frappes and root beer floats! They
were thrilled! They showed Fiona's picture to the waitresses,
and they muttered among themselves as they kept looking back at them. It was kind of obvious they recognized

Fiona. Tony became anxious to find his daughter; he felt they were getting closer. His knee was bouncing up and down a hundred miles hour as he tapped his hands on the table, as though he were playing the drums. Their waitress saw this and headed back to their table.

"Here's your picture," she said as she placed it on the table along with the bill in front of Tony.

"Have you seen her?" Tony asked quickly with great enthusiasm.

"I'm not sure," she replied, "I'm just not sure. She kind of looks familiar, but I'm not sure. I'm sorry."

Tony immediately replied, "I'll tell you what," he said, "we'll come back in a couple of days. Just keep an eye out for her, will you? Can you do that for us? Please? I'm her father Tony, and these are my two sons, Don and Tom. And her mother back home in Massachusetts is devastated. We're all worried about her and we need to find her. She may be in trouble. Will you help us?" he pleaded as he caught his breath and held back the tears. The waitress sighed, agreeing to keep an eye out for her. Tony told her that they would be back in two days as he held two fingers up so there would be no confusion. They returned to the car hoping that this would become a good lead to find Fiona. Tony drove them directly back to Woody's Back Door Lounge. He parked the car up the road and around the corner. It had a good view of the dive. Deep down they were all hoping they wouldn't see her in a place like this. But the three of them sat in the car in complete silence and alert, watching without a blink or wink. Every kind of savory character you can think of went in and out of that place, excessive traffic.

Tony and the boys knew damn well that they would be devoured if they dared enter that place. It became very late, but Donny insisted that they wait it out even if it meant taking shifts to sleep and be on the lookout. He had high hopes of finding her here.

They gave up as the night became day. They'd return to the hotel room, again without Fiona, which was very upsetting to them. They were tired and hungry and irritable. Tony laid down on the bed and fell asleep the moment his head hit the pillow. His loud snoring made the boys chuckle as they joined him and also laid down.

When they awoke, they were facing a new day well-rested. And still hungry. They decided to walk to the IHOP down the street for some breakfast, in the hopes of finding a lead to Fiona's whereabouts. But they came up with nothing. Afterward, they walked the streets showing her photo, approaching everyone desperately seeking the truth. Nobody anywhere had seen Fiona and that was that. Tony broke down, covering his face with his hands, holding his head in agony and defeat. He had trusted her. Never seeing his sweet Fiona again was too bitter of a pill for Tony to swallow. He regained his composure for his sons' sakes.

They still had to return to the IHOP the next day to talk to that waitress. There was a small ray of hope, like the sun peeking through the clouds. Tony had a tiny shred of hope, but at the back of his mind he thought that he was only fooling himself. Did his best to show it. He did not want his sons to lose another sister, their only sister, the baby of the family. He couldn't fathom the thought.

Suddenly Tony caught a glimpse of his waitress from the comer of his eye. She was knocking on the window, looking right at him, and waving her hand to tell him to come back in. So Tony did just that.

"She wants to tell me something," Tony said with much optimism. "You guys wait out here, and don't take your eyes off of me." Tony walked back into the IHOP restaurant and went directly to the waitress.

"Did you remember something?" he asked her politely.

"Nobody can know that I talked to you," she muttered, looking Tony square in the eye.

"Fine, fine," Tony replied, crossing his heart, "I won't tell a soul, I promise!"

"There's an old house four blocks from here. It still has a plastic Halloween skeleton decoration hanging on the front door. You can't miss it," she whispered to him. "It's a condemned house, it has a big X on it, but Buzz does his business in there selling drugs your little heart desires. People get so messed up in there that most of them don't bother leaving. Just like the Hotel California, you can come, but you can never leave." She sung briefly and continued, "Sly works for this Buzz guy. Everyone in there calls it home, you get my drift?" she asked Tony.

"Yeah, yeah, what's this got to do with my daughter?" Tony asked her outwardly.

"Buzz made her his number one girl! She helps him unload too much merchandise. I'm talking quantities, you following me?" the waitress asked.

"Yes, thank you for this information, Sally," Tony replied as he read her name tag. "Thank you very much," he continued gratefully and gracefully. Then she warned him to be very careful, because Buzz was untouchable and unstoppable and indestructible! And also, Buzz was very successful at manipulating young girls who've lost their way, and getting them hooked so they'd become loyal to him. The waitress continued, "If anyone asks, say that you, Tony, was asking me for directions to Disneyland and retrieving the keys you left on the table." They both agreed, and Tony turned around leaving her. He held his jacket closed, protecting himself from the wind as he dodged the traffic, crossing the street to return to his two sons who were still waiting for him as they watched his every move, never taking their eyes off of him. He was excited to tell them some news of what he had just learned, and they were excited to have some hope.

Tony told them, "There's an abandoned house four blocks from here, and Fiona may be in it!" He continued to tell them the whole story, and they were ready to accompany their father to this "broken-down palace" holding their sister captive. They all knew without saying that there must be some drugs involved after hearing what they'd just heard. They returned to the car that was parked around the comer, and began their quest in search of their beloved Fiona. Tony braced himself for the worst, praying for strength. They came upon the house they believed Fiona to be in, and were appalled at the condition of the house even though they knew it was condemned.

They didn't ever expect it to be this bad. The two-story house was covered in vines and moss, and there was even a huge hole in the roof, not to mention that half the roof was missing! Some windows were broken and some were gone completely. The place looked haunted to say the least, especially with a Halloween skeleton still on the door! It was the end of July! The shrubs were overgrown, covering the front entrance sidewalk leading to the front door. They were certain that they had the right place.

They stayed in the car, waiting for someone to leave or arrive, hoping to see Fiona. Hours went by as they waited in anticipation for some kind of sign. And then, finally, after the sunset, they began seeing some action when a crowd of people arrived on foot and entered the drug house. There were a total of six people. And then two people came out of the house and onto the porch, and both of them lit cigarettes to smoke. When they were finished, they stumbled back inside the house.

More time passed by before they began to give up. Dad, Donny said boldly, "we can't even see, it is so dark, what the hell are we doing?" Before he could continue, the three of them held their breath as they watched someone of small stature, dressed in all black, wearing a black baseball cap, nonchalantly go inside the old abandoned two-story condemned house as the screen door, hanging on one hinge, slammed. Tony remembered when Fee used to slam the door, he'd welcome it now. They couldn't tell if it was Fiona or not. It could've been a guy, a very puny man, if a man. It was hard to tell; they really couldn't see or say for sure. Tony, Donny, and Tommy looked at each other simultaneously, all knowing that now was their chance to make their move. They got out of the car quietly so that they wouldn't be noticed. Tony and the boys crossed the street walking toward the abandoned house. They entered. There were people on the floor almost stopping the front door from opening. They were out of it! But they tried to make room for the door to open. Once they all got past the front door, they stood there and listened. They wanted to hear Fiona's voice among the crowd, but all they heard was moaning from this one or that one. They had no choice but to search the entire house. They were uncomfortable stepping over bodies lying everywhere, but they didn't have a choice. They were just going to have to do it in hopes of finding Fiona! There was no sign of her among all these obvious homeless drug addicts.

A lot of them just scored whatever was their drug of choice, because they were perking up, starting the cycle all over again! Many of them would huddle around who-ever bought something from the pusher. "God damn the pusher!" They looked like a flock of pigeons in the park congregating around the guy feeding them from the park bench! It was pitiful! Tony and Don and Tom just looked at each other. There were no words to speak. They were so out of their element!

"Let's try upstairs," Tony stated. "I'd at least like to know if that was Fiona that entered the house *as* we all watched, all dressed in black." It was apparent to them that nobody here acknowledged their presence. It was heart-wrenching for them to see. Young people, old people, living from one fix to the next! There was a young girl all curled up in a comer who resembled Fiona. She was curled up in a ball, and it was obvious that she was going through withdrawals. She was crying and shaking, sweating profusely. All she was wearing was a clear plastic garbage bag.

Tony and his sons were deeply affected by what they saw. They would never forget it. They figured she must've sold her clothes for a fix, for stuff, or she forgot them somewhere or left them—or lost them. It was hard to see. That image would forever be stamped on their minds.

They had to walk away, they just couldn't take it! Tony gestured to the boys to follow him up the stairs, so they did. They were careful to place each foot gently between the bodies congregated on the steps leading to the second floor. It appeared to them that this crowd was used to it. But when they arrived at the top step, they came to a halt. A man stood right in front of them. He was elderly. His face was hidden by his long, scraggly gray hair. His beard was long and bushy. He looked like he had never showered, but he looked sober compared to the lot of them. He stared at Tony and the boys, as if they needed a password or something get by him. Tony didn't know what to make of it, so he took a chance and continued to the old man, and his sons followed. The old guy never flinched. He just stared right through the three of them, staring into space as though they weren't even there. Once they got around him, they tiptoed down the dark hallway, listening for Fiona's voice. Every room was occupied. There were people everywhere! It was so sad! The smells were downright nasty. Body odors lingered in the smoke-filled rooms, floating in the air. The boys were uncomfortable being there, Tony as well.

"Dad, we should go," Tommy said nervously.

"All right, we only have one room left to check, and then we'll get the hell out of here!" he replied. So they proceeded to the last room. They entered the room together, and much to their surprise, they ran into the person all dressed in black whom they saw enter the house earlier. This person was pushing the drugs since entering the house. It was Fiona! She turned around startled. She shoved the cash in her pants pocket, and looked at the three of them as though they were strangers! When they tried to approach her to hug her, she shrugged them off as though it was forbidden.

"Fiona! It's me, Dad," he pleaded as she pulled away. "We have to get you out of here, honey, you're in great danger!"

"You're crazy!" she replied, "I've got it made! I'm doing fine, really!" Fiona stated plainly. Tony went back and forth with her, making his case to her to come back home where she belonged, where she's loved by all the family and friends there. But she resisted as though she had been brainwashed! She kept right on refusing to change for she loved her lifestyle. She wasn't held captive; she actually liked her lifestyle! And she wasn't going to take any shit! Even when her brothers pleaded with her to come home with them, she refused. They felt so sad and helpless. It was like a death in the family, all over again! Tony wasn't about to give up that easily. Tony tried again to chat and reason with his daughter, but Fiona wasn't having it! It was as though love were forbidden, in fear of becoming too soft. Then Tony pulled her aside to talk with her without her brothers present.

"Fiona, please," Tony pleaded, holding her close to him, "I can't leave you here like this! You're a mess!" he said shaking, with tears in his eyes. "Surely you must be hungry? And I bet you'd love a nice hot shower, wouldn't you, Fiona? Let me help you."

"I don't need any help!" Fiona replied as she shrugged away from him. "Besides, everything I need is right here in California!"

"But, honey, do you have a home out here? With a bed and all that?" Tony asked.

"I don't need one out here. The weather is always warm, and I can lay down on the beach if I want to when I'm tired, or I can stay over at Buzz's place. He would do just about anything for me," Fiona stated. Tony could feel his blood pressure rising just from hearing Buzz's name.

Fiona shouted at Tony. "Time is money!" Then she ran down the stairs, out of the house, and out of sight, just like that.

"He's using you, Fiona! Can't you see that?" Tony screamed, holding his head tightly in his hands, then throwing his arms up in the air, motioning surrender. Tony was fit to be tied as he broke down and landed on his knees. He broke down with his face in hands, trying to hide his tears. "Dear God!" he shouted. "Help us!" He pleaded as he wiped his tears away, regaining strength and composure. He got up and turned to his sons and said, "We've lost her. We've lost her." He unsuccessfully held his tears back. Don and Tom each grabbed an arm of their father as they gently escorted him out of the condemned crack house. The three of them remained completely silent, feeling defeated. They didn't know where she ran off to, or why she would ever run from them. Their heads hung low. "I don't know what to do," Tony stated as they approached the car. "Do we walk away?" he cried. "Maybe we should be looking for Buzz?"

"Dad, we don't know how dangerous this guy is!" Tom said.

"Of course he's dangerous!" Tony yelled angrily.

"Let me drive," Donny said, holding his hand out for the car keys from his father.

"I'll sit in the back," Tony said, slamming the door shut. Don drove around downtown browsing through the crowds on the sidewalks. Tommy concentrated on the thick, congested crowds huddled together waiting to cross the street at the instant of a green signal to cross. Tony remained silent in the back seat as he prayed for guidance on his next move, thinking if he was wrong to take this into his own hands. Shouldn't he trust God to handle it? But doesn't God help those who help themselves? The more he dwelt on these questions, the more he felt torn. "Let's just go back to the hotel, Don," Tony said. "I need a break."

"You got it, Dad," Don replied. Later, they all took a shower to get ready to go out and get something for supper. After taking turns scrubbing away the devil's vileness they encountered, their appetites grew. There was a Red Robin restaurant directly across the street from the hotel they were staying at, so they walked there. When they walked into the restaurant, it was very busy. They were seated right away. In the center of the restaurant, there was an oversized birdcage which housed two lovebirds. They were beautiful, quite the focal point. It took Tony back in time, to where he and Martha began the same way, in such simpler times. The three of them were happy to see the alcohol menu and all ordered a drink to calm their nerves. They were so very worried about Fiona and still felt uneasy. There were few words spoken, although they had similar thoughts.

It was time for them to pull over and out of the fast lane. It could've become dangerous, more than they could handle. It was a most unfamiliar world to them, without rules. They began to consider themselves lucky. They were still together and none of them were hurt. They hoped they didn't get Fiona in trouble. They now knew what happened to Fiona.

But it wasn't closure. And they knew it. They spent two hours at Red Robin as they enjoyed relaxing and taking a look at things from a distance. When they left the restaurant, they agreed to take a walk farther down the road to walk off their supper. They stayed close so they wouldn't get separated in the rushing crowds. They were like fish out of water, in an unfamiliar world. They were certainly country folk compared to all these city folk.

There was so much to look at between signs of businesses or products, and strange people to look at as well, from all walks of life! But they had enough of it and decided to tum back before they went too far. They turned around after crossing the street, heading back toward the hotel. Walking past a bus stop, they overheard a scrawny kid in the phone booth repeating the same thing over and over again.

"Okay, Buzz…okay, yes, okay!" he yelled. The kid looked hungry and strung out. He kept taking off his black ball cap and wiping his brow off with his ripped shirt, which you couldn't tell was once white. He reeked of perspiration, and his eyes looked dead. Tony couldn't help himself. He was compelled to stop and talk to this kid. He signaled his boys to stop at the comer and wait for him there. He walked over to the kid slowly, acting like he was also there waiting for the bus. When the kid hung up the phone and came out of the phone booth, Tony made his move.

"I couldn't help but overhear that you know Buzz too, huh? Well, this has to be the same guy? How many Buzzes can there be?" Tony laughed, keeping his cool.

"Yeah, right," the kid answered.

"Are you on your way to see him too?" Tony asked. The boy nodded in confirmation. Tony offered him a twenty-dollar bill for information about Buzz and where he resides. But at the same time, the bus was pulling up, getting louder the closer it got, the brakes squeaking so loud you couldn't hear yourself think! All the people waiting for the bus began to hustle and bustle with impatience and rudeness. The boy got up to get on the bus and Tony cried, "Don't go! Let me buy you some new sneakers, and then maybe you could give me information? I'm just trying to find my daughter." Tony was at his mercy. The kid looked down at his feet and at his sneakers that were so old they looked like they were literally held together by the shoelaces! His big toes were starting to poke a hole right through. He looked back up at Tony.

"There's another bus in fifteen minutes," he reported. Tony was so grateful to him that he gave him another twenty-dollar bill, asking him a question.

"Do you have any information that can help me to find my daughter, Fiona?" He held up her picture, and the boy gazed at it. And then he looked at Tony, and then looked at the picture again.

"What is it?" Tony asked anxiously. And the poor boy replied hesitantly.

"Well, she kind of looks like somebody that Buzz has working for him, but her name is Scarlett. And her hair is black, not brown." Tony had just seen her with her black hair and he knew that she changed her hair color frequently like the seasons change.

"But what about her face?" Tony asked in desperation. "Does it look like her?"

"Yeah," the boy said, "I got to admit, it looks just like her!"

"Will you take me to her?" Tony asked the kid as he held his breath waiting for the answer.

"I'd love to, but nobody gets to her or to Buzz unless they can get past Rafael. He protects them and the whole network basically." He went on to tell Tony that the only way he'll ever find his daughter is if he lives the same lifestyle as her and that it could be years before she surfaces again. "Because the word is out that you and two others have been seen snooping around, to find her, and Buzz isn't happy. Now Buzz has her in hiding until you guys disappear. Even if she sneaks about, she knows the game and how not to get caught, especially now that she knows you're here. All I can tell you is good luck!" He then removed his hat and used his sleeve to wipe the sweat off his brow.

"Thanks," Tony replied. Tony reached into his pants pocket and pulled out another twenty-dollar bill and held it up in front of the kid's face. "This is yours if you can tell me anything else that would help me." Staring at each other, Tony slowly handed the twenty-dollar bill to the boy, who took it from him and tucked it away inside his hat.

"All I can tell you is, if you don't leave, there's going to be serious trouble. Real trouble! They won't think twice about killing any of you! The more you chase her, the more she will run! Go home, and wait for her to return to you. If she does or if she doesn't, it is her choice! Right now, she is safe. Why would you want to put her in danger and in harm's way? Leave the area now before you need an army to protect you! This thing is much bigger than you are!" The boy was through giving his advice to Tony, and looked on toward the bus that was coming to a stop. He picked up his skateboard and he walked away from Tony into the crowds of people, disappearing so fast that Tony wasn't even sure that the kid got on the bus or not. He looked across the street and saw his two sons, Don and Tom, were still there patiently waiting for him. When they approached Tony, they had many questions. They saw the whole thing and figured out dear old dad must've gotten a lot of information because he talked with that kid for a long time. But they were surprised at Tony's response. The only thing that he said to his boys was that it was time for them all to go home, realizing that it was in God's hands. Tony filled the boys in on Fiona being fooled into selling her body because this loser guy "Buzz" was her pimp and pusher all in one! He renamed her Scarlett! Of course, the boys wanted to go after this creep Buzz who was destroying their sister. But Tony warned them about Buzz. He was no one to fool with!

He was a big, husky guy, not the most handsome thing, but he managed to put a spell on Fiona. Correction, Scarlett. The guy was a loser with a capital L. He was a high school dropout who could barely handle minimum-wage jobs, lacking education. Buzz used to jump around from one job to another, never getting anywhere.

His bodyguard was Rafael, and his number one runner was Sly. That's right, Sly, he's a guy who doesn't matter to Rafael.

Buzz supposedly had a kid somewhere in Iowa, whom he didn't give a shit about. Buzz always ran from his child support responsibilities and obligations and neglected his daughter. His probation officer was on his tail, and that's really why he was so hard to find. Buzz was a pussy under his tough-guy facade, a big pussy who liked to bully women and make them hustle just to give him the money. And he kept them high on a multitude of different street drugs. Buzz didn't even have an apartment! He squatted in an abandoned building downtown that had an old elevator with the gate covering the door that ran manually, just like the one back at that hotel where Fiona and Rachael had stayed at in Vegas. The ceilings were two floors high in the big industrial brick building where Buzz squatted. It still had old machines in there that looked like it once made fabrics or did weaving. The cobwebs covered them atop the foot of dust, but over in the comer was Buzz's little pad. And that was the only information that Tony had gotten from the kid.

Don and Tommy tried to talk to their father into finding this place and grabbing Fiona, and then getting the hell out of there! But Tony knew that it just wasn't that easy. Instead, he told them both that they could stay another day or so, just to see if they'd run into her where they thought she'd be working for Buzz. But they wouldn't be ambushing anybody thought to be dangerous on his watch! The three of them agreed to get a fresh start in the morning. Tony was sure that their cover was blown wide open, and looking for her tonight would just make her run farther. He hoped that if they laid low for the night, they would suspect that he and the boys must've given up and packed up and left.

His plan did work a couple of days later, because Buzz and "Scarlett" were back to business as usual. They had both assumed just that—that they gave up and left town. And word was out on the streets that Tony and his sons were long gone because they were nowhere to be found. Tony prayed that withdrawing for the night would pay off. It did, because everyone working the streets let their guard down and returned to their so-called comfort zone.

Tony didn't sleep a wink. He worried so much about his daughter being in danger like that every day and being manipulated by this creep! He was just using her! And he found it unreal that anyone could be successful at manipulating Fiona in the first place! Tony could hardly believe it possible! She was so independent and strong-willed. Martha called it pigheaded. Then his mind wandered and tried to picture his own daughter living like this, running from crack house to crack house, using and seeing her action shooting up and worse in his mind's eye. He couldn't wrap his head around it! He had to stop it! He couldn't take it anymore!

He jumped up and out of bed and stared out the window into the darkness of the night, waiting for morning to arrive. He prayed again to God for strength and help and guidance to save his daughter. He couldn't bear losing two daughters. He had never dealt with or gotten past losing Tori, and his heart couldn't handle any more heartache. His heart hurt, physically. He felt like the weakest on earth at that moment. But somehow, he found inner strength, and he wiped his tears away and dried his eyes once more, concentrating on starting a fresh new day with high hopes. He wanted to stay positive, he had to for the boy's sake. He could see the toll it was taking on them. They loved Fiona. She was special to them. And they too were overprotective with her; they were just like Martha that way. And for good reason.

Fiona was a live wire, always taking chances, seeking thrills, never fearing anything or anyone. But in this case, she had been outsmarted by the lowest of the lowliest! Tony knew deep down that in Fiona's defense, she was feeling independent and at first it was just partying, and it crept up on her; it could happen to anybody, turn into a lifestyle. *But that's no life,* Tony thought. Tommy and Donny woke up one after the other, ripping farts and laughing that their asses were their alarm clocks! Tony's eyes were running and he was gasping for air they stunk so bad! Tommy paced the floor since Don beat him to the bathroom.

"Dad, are you all right?" Tom asked, still chuckling. Tony looked him in the eye when he said he was doing all right. Clearly the tone in his voice revealed how upset he was about Fiona. His daughter had been debased, giving him a feeling of ignominy, as her life ebbs away. Buzz's denizens of death were upon her, causing her to lag, no longer bent and all zeal gone.

Tony knew it was out of his own power that this calamity could he fixed and made right. By this time, Donny and Tommy were ready to hit the streets wanting to annihilate this Buzz guy! Tony lauded them for their confidence, and the gregarious three were seated in their panacea fantasy. They felt like a roaring conflagration ready to consume anything and anyone in its path. And Tony, well, he could sense and feel the devil's presence smack in the middle of his daughter's life. He informed the boys that his plan was to go to that Halloween costume shop that he saw yesterday near the cluster of palm trees over by the park and get something for them to wear as a disguise. Maybe they'd have better luck here while in disguise, rather than being recognized and scaring her off into hiding. Tom and Don loved the idea, and the three left the hotel immediately.

When they entered the costume store, they were overwhelmed with how big the place was inside. There was every kind of costume you could think of, on three floors counting the basement. There were gypsy outfits and clown outfits, cowboys and Indians, superheroes, Casper the friendly ghost, and they even had H. R. Pufnstuf! You name it, they had it. And witches and gory, bloody costumes, including shelves upon shelves of masks of heads with bloody cleavers in their head and sliced throats bleeding profusely, rotten teeth look which Tom spotted and suggested to look like your average junky, as he put it. He also found himself a floppy, old red hat made of felt that looked ancient, but yet was like new. He grabbed a wig to wear under the hat, which had messy long hair with tangles from hell. So he had his red hat and long hair of a rat's nest and rotten teeth.

Tom was all set with his getup, and when he rang up his purchase at the register, he threw in a pair sunglasses. Tony and Donny were still looking around, while Tom put on all of the stuff he bought and was now in disguise. He told them that he would wait for them inside while trying out his new look.

Don spotted some hippy looks and was excited to do some. He saw an outfit that came as a set, with old-looking bell-bottom jeans, a striped shirt with florescent, psychedelic colors, and a raggedy looking purple velvet vest with long fringes. There was a wig full of a Rastafarian braids, and a pair of tiny round spectacles just big enough to hide his eyeballs. Tony finally settled for the heavy metal look. He found an outfit that was all black leather. It came with a black leather vest and chaps to match and to wear over his jeans, with black leather gloves with all the fingers cut off just showing the fingertips, and a wide red bandana to wear across his forehead. He tied it in a knot in the back of his head.

Don couldn't stop laughing at Tony as he held his purchase, waiting for his turn to cash out. Tony couldn't help but laugh with him. It was good to laugh. They both agreed that nobody would recognize them. In fact, when they left the store and stepped out onto the busy sidewalk, Tommy said he would have never recognized either one of them if he hadn't overheard their voices when they came out laughing and teasing each other.

Tommy had been outside waiting while watching all the people hustle and bustle on the sidewalks and streets, racing for the crosswalk, while some took their sweet old time. Nobody ever noticed him while he waited outside for Don and Tony. He thoroughly enjoyed being in disguise in his long, tangled hair, with his floppy hat and dark sunglasses and rotten teeth. It made him feel courageous. It made him feel eager to blend in with the rest that surrounded him. Tom was feeling ballsy and was ready for the hunt. The three of them talked it out about their next move in attempts to devise a plan. They did know that they couldn't stand there together looking obvious.

Tony chose to go across the street to hang around and scope out the scenery. His two boys were still in sight, which made Tony feel better. He was quite nervous. This kind of lifestyle was foreign to Tony, which he thanked his lucky stars for, and he knew the streets were a dangerous place. Awful thoughts crept into his mind about Fiona's existence, and why, oh why, would this appeal to her? And then he realized, while walking, really realizing, just how sick my baby girl is. His little girl was gone. Even if it turned out well, he knew the Fiona he once knew would be never more. The old Fiona was gone. She's gone forever! But he had to find her. He just had to give it one more shot. Donny and Tommy both felt the same way.

He could still see them across the street. He watched as Don went into the Circle K, and he came out with a new pack of cigarettes and lit one up, and he didn't even smoke. But he was trying to portray a hippie and thought smoking would help. He's lucky his Rastafarian dreadlocks didn't go up in smoke with the dirty butt hanging out of his face, while the white smoke filled behind his tiny round spectacles and gave the same look you get with dry ice. He sure did look like a cool dude in a loose mood! He "shot the shit" or "chewed the fat" briefly with folks as they'd walk by him, experiencing how people treated him different because of the way he looked, grasping what it's like on the other side of the fence, so to speak. Then Tony too noticed Tommy was moving farther down the street and was in line to buy some popcorn from a vendor. When he was done, he walked over to a bench by the bus stop and sat down to enjoy eating it. Tom got caught up in feeding some to the pigeons as he scoped things out, searching for a sign that would lead them to Fiona.

They knew Fiona's alias name was Scarlett, and they knew this Buzz scumbag controlled her, and he was a very dangerous man with nothing to lose. He manipulated women, making them his slaves to do his dirty work since he was too good to work as if above it. He was in charge of the streets and his territory, and had his rules to follow, or else. His own network of mules pushed his goods of an abundant assortment. He was hardened and held an impressive list of arrests since dropping out of high school sophomore year. His mom was a crackhead, and who knows who or where his dad was? They would have to be careful when they found this creep. Tommy thought he heard someone drop the name Scarlett as they walked by him as he sat on the bench eating his popcorn. He turned to give Tony a look of surprise, as he raised his eyebrows and his mouth hung wide open. Tony saw his cue, so he walked toward Tom in the same direction as Tom nodded his head to keep going, directing him nonchalantly in attempts to stay inconspicuous and unnoticed. The stranger walking by who dropped the name Scarlett was just a young kid.

Tony had noticed the kid stop walking to talk to a group of young people just hanging out together gathered on the street comer. Tony had no choice but to keep walking past them so he wouldn't blow his cover. He was kind of noticeable with that bright red bandana and leather getup, looking like a badass biker or something. Don threw his cigarette on the ground, stomping it out with his hippie sandals, and started walking toward the crowd of kids loitering together.

Among them was Rafael, Scarlett's personal assistant! He was supposedly there to protect her and keep her safe. He was also Sly's pimp. But where is she? Don recognized Rafael from the last time he saw his sister Fiona on the street. He knew it was the same guy, he was sure of it! Rafael wore a sleeveless white Tshirt with white shorts, and a gray shirt that he wrapped around his waist and into a knot, the sleeves of which went hanging off of him in the front, all stretched out, and he had the most faded tattoo of a skull on his left forearm which Don had ever seen. Don was sure it was Rafael; he was wearing the same clothes! He was sure of it. He started looking for Fiona. Don walked past Rafael, standing with his friends huddled in a circle, and crossed the side street and continued walking slowly looking into the windows of every mall business or food joint. The streets were busy with businessmen and women rushing with their briefcases as they ran, walked, and some women were walking their kids to school pushing carriages, and work crews were working on putting in a new sidewalk on the opposite side of the main road. The UPS trucks and buses stopped at red lights, with their awfully loud screechy brakes. There were cab drivers beeping their horns for no apparent reason. Don stopped walking and sat on the grass when he approached a very small park with really no attractions, just a good spot for a break. He didn't want to lose his brother Tom, or his father Tony. He tried to look back for them, but the streets were full of people, and he walked quite a ways ahead of them. Donny figured he'd been walking for twenty to thirty minutes, and that's why he decided not to go any farther.

Tommy was still near the costume store, and he could see Rafael and his group of friends loitering outside of the music store, and Tony was also still in his view, even though he was across the street. Tom thought, *How clever of Dad to cross the street virtually unnoticed, with a full view of them all.* Tony could see how antsy and restless Rafael was. Tony was hoping that Rafael wasn't on to them. Suddenly, Tony saw Fiona coming in the near distance, and he flagged Tom to wait and stay put.

So Tom did just that, and Fiona walked right by him without ever recognizing her own brother—still in disguise, of course—with his rotten teeth and that floppy red hat and psychedelic shirt. Tom also thought, *My god, what a mess she is, and dirty, with a stinky rat's nest for hair, and ratty clothes, and a big handbag made of patchwork patches hanging from her shoulder.* Her right hand stayed in the bag as she walked along, stopping to talk to Rafael and his following, his little clan. So Tommy figured he would fit right in with this poverty-stricken bum costume with the long, tangled hair, rotten teeth, broken glasses, grungy dirty-looking clothes, and that floppy old hat. He was ready to blend in with the others. But Tony nonchalantly warned him not to move, so he didn't.

By this time, Don had backtracked enough to see his father in plain sight. But Tom couldn't see his brother Don, and Don couldn't see him. But luckily, Tony could see both his sons, and Rafael and Fiona and everyone. Tony signaled Don to wait also. They could see the deals going down, lots of exchanges with Fiona's involvement in every one of them, with her bag of tricks at close hand. Rafael hung around until they all got what they were waiting for, and then he got what he wanted. All the loot! They could see that it looked like she was giving him instructions as Rafael paid close attention to what she was saying, and suddenly they separated, and Rafael crossed the street disappearing into the crowd. Tony signaled the boys to go after Fiona who was slipping away into a side street. Don and Tom started running after her, until they cornered her in a dead-end alley, surrounded by tall brick buildings with clotheslines and clothes hanging above. It also housed numerous trash bins overflowing with garbage. Fiona stopped, turning around abruptly, as her hippy beads swung around her tiny malnutritioned body, making a clanking sound.

"What's your problem?!" Fiona screamed. "I just have to press one button, and Rafael will be all over you! What the hell do you want?" she continued, feeling panicky, knowing she was in danger with these strangers because she didn't have any buttons to press to call Rafael. She was bluffing. And Buzz wasn't going to save her; if anything, he would punish her. "Why are you cornering me like this? Let me out of here!" she said agitated. "I'm sold out, so you guys are shit out of luck!" Tom and Don had her cornered, while Tony caught up and joined them quickly. He took a good look at his daughter. She was unrecognizable to him. His eyes welled up as he took another gander at her. "What the hell do you want, big boy?" Fiona said warily as he approached her.

"It's me, Fiona," Tony said, suspecting she would know his voice. But she didn't. Tony couldn't believe it!

"I don't know you, or Fiona! My name is Scarlett!" she screamed at him furiously.

"It's me, Dad," Tony said softly, reaching for her hands. She pulled away, crying and stomping her feet angrily.

"No!" she yelled. "My name is Scarlett! Get away from me, you have the wrong person!" she pleaded as she pulled her hands away and stepped back. Her denial of herself seemed to be torturing her as she whimpered on.

"Fiona, stop it," Tony said softly and as gently as possible. "We miss you, sweetheart. Your mother is beside herself, we all love you so much!"

"Yeah, Fiona, I miss you, man!" Donny told her as he stepped up to stand closer to her. She gazed at him in his hippy getup, until she was looking directly at him, recognizing him.

"And I miss you like crazy too, Fee!" Tommy said with a weak smile. Fiona broke down, overwhelmed by her father and her two brothers' presence. It was too much for her to handle; she felt like a trapped rat looking to make a run for it. She was feeling claustrophobic. They could see that what they were saying was finally starting to penetrate. She had to escape, like always. She couldn't breathe. Tony held her arms and pulled her to himself, holding her as she cried. Don and Tom pulled in closer and they had a group hug lasting at least a minute, as everyone sighed with relief. They found Fiona! Of course, Tony and the boys figured it was finally over, but in fact Fiona, or Scarlett, knew different. There was so much more to it! It just wasn't that easy!

"Okay!" Fiona screamed, raising her arms, putting them together over her head as she dropped them to get away from them. "That's enough! I got to go before Buzz sends his goons after me," she stated matter-of-factly. "It was very nice to see you all, but I have to go, for real!" She stomped. But they wouldn't have it, and got in her face.

"You have to come with us, Fee! You can't stay here," Tony insisted, "we'll help you every step of the way." She broke free of them and ran out of the alley never looking back. Into the crowded street she disappeared, never to be seen again. All the love and prayers could not save her. Accepting that fact was a hard pill to swallow!

Tori's tears flowed like rain from the clouds, and suddenly, it was pouring in LA. Tony had never felt such a loss as this, an empty pit in the core of his being. So terribly defeated. He asked God for strength to get through this trial. His little girl was gone. Donny and Tom were angry. They couldn't believe it! But after Tony sat them down and calmed them, they all came to the same conclusion. Fiona wouldn't come back home unless she wanted to. Only Fiona could make that decision. God gave everyone the freedom of choice. Perhaps this is the reason why the world is such a mess.

The following morning, they checked out of Motel 6 and headed home to Martha. They dreaded telling her that Fiona wasn't coming home. This was the hardest thing Tony would have to do. The long drive back home made it a comfort for them to reflect and process everything that happened. It was a unanimous vote to take turns driving and not sleep anywhere.

When they finally saw that *Welcome to Massachusetts* sign, they were relieved, excited, and a little anxious, and had that awful feeling you get when you have to tell somebody terrible news. Tony and the boys made it back home okay. Martha was relieved that they were finally back, and she could now stop worrying. They went on with their lives, but there was always a scent in the air of the loss they all felt with Fiona, and the aftertaste of the wonderful memories of her when she blossomed and bloomed and brightened everyone's day, bringing life and light to the room. And now they had to learn how to accept the things that they could not change. Patience, understanding, hope, wisdom, love. They had lost her long ago.

Martha always expected the worst about everything. She was a pessimist. She always thought that way, so that she would always be prepared. But she found out differently this time. They all went on with their lives the best way they knew how. Martha would get updates from Rachael about Fiona, who kept in touch with Rachael. Rachael had informed Fiona that she heard who Mickey Melouin got pregnant when he cheated. He cheated with Sequoia Mathews, the tag-a-long friend, and they had a daughter together, Sophia Marie, same age as Tommy and Felicia's little one, Victoria. Victoria was the spitting image of her aunt Fiona, two peas in a pod. She blossomed and bloomed, brightening everyone's day, bringing life and light to the room, just like her auntie.

When Fiona heard about Sequoia and Mickey and their daughter, she was very upset and scarred. She was fooled again by someone she trusted. And Sequoia told Fiona to her face that she knew he had been cheating on Fiona, but she never said who it was! And it was her! But Fiona knew all this before she fled to California from her troubles, and she wasn't ever coming back, affecting all who loved her. All updates stopped when Rachael ended up going back to California.

Donny and Tommy would take trips to Los Angeles once a year, in hopes of finding Fiona and bringing her home. But they never found her again. Was she dead or alive? No one knew. They had to learn how to live without her. They lived with the hope that maybe one day Fiona would walk through that door. Until then, they prayed and kept the faith. The entire family stayed connected and pulled together. They protected their very souls with reasoning, trusting their hearts and their minds, living with integrity, no strife, doing what they said, and doing everything with excellence. And they were blessed.

Tommy and Felicia and their daughter Victoria went on to live happily ever after. Despite the heartbreak Tommy went through losing his sidekick, Fiona, he managed to keep his playful demeanor. He clowned around and tickled and teased his daughter Vicki and Felicia, and played tricks on them, always making them laugh and smile. Tommy's contagious smile and grin always tipped the others off of his eagerness to pull something off, every chance he got. He saw so much of Fiona in his daughter, Victoria, her mannerisms and expressions, and the attitude of independence. There was also the bright light within her that illuminated within her, which was the same light Fiona once had.

Donny immersed himself in his work, which he enjoyed so much. He became a great success. He eventually married and had some kids of his own. He spent the majority of his time traveling for his work, flying all over the world, doing his job. Martha and Tony never got to see him much due to his excessive traveling. But he always stayed in touch, and they always made it to the family reunions.

Martha and Tony enjoyed the kids and the grandkids, and at every gathering they knew they were truly blessed.

Eventually, Tony got sick again and his legs were amputated because of the diabetes. And then, not long afterward, he passed, losing his battle and will to live, never seeing his Fiona again. When Fiona didn't come home for his funeral, despite knowing about his passing through Rachael's mom, people asked who now would keep her informed. The family pulled together, and life marched on without her. Her brothers decided to stop going to California once a year to try and locate her. It was like two deaths in the family.

Collectively, they lived life as it was dealt to them, and stayed in faith for the rest of their lives, living in love, peace, harmony, patience, and trust.

Martha had a poem that she often quoted, "Love is cure":

> Love is power,
> Love is the magic of changes,
> Love is the mirror of divine beauty."
> —Rumi

Tori always kept an eye on Fiona, but her abilities were being restrained, learning too that God was in charge and in control, and to believe in him and his will. With God's will, run the race to the finish line and claim your promised prize.